# Lion Ascend

By

Ryan Keith Johnson

All songs, poems via compositions are written by the author, Ryan Keith Johnson

Compositions can be found in the book "What I Think About You" except
I'll Catch You
Hold You Like A Memory
Moon Cheetah

ISBN    978-0-615-53086-4

I would like to dedicate this story to Corrine (Cheetah).
May all your dreams come true.

# Lion Ascend

"It began with the great lions; the protectors of peace throughout the land. For thousands of years the lions united Ayana in harmony, until evil possessed the tigers to invade and conquer the land. The tigers did not share the way of life that the lions created.

For hundreds of years, war raged between the lions and the tigers. A division was created and the animals had to decide who to follow. The lion's numbers appeared to be declining while the tigers looked like they were winning. The animals were forced to choose sides in order to survive.

To end the war; Prince Voltar led his army to the lions' resting places and killed them in their sleep. One by one the cubs never found their courage and became weak as they grew older. Some abandoned their future and ran away to the outer reaches of Everlow. The few lions, which were left to face the tigers' wrath were killed. Through their deaths, Prince Voltar let out a loud roar declaring that would be born not of Ayana. He would lead the fight for freedom of all the animals from the treachery of the tigers. He would have a thunderous roar and would run as fast as a night mare as well as fight a hundred tigers combined. The animals would unite and stand with him against evil!

With this information, I began spreading the news to all the animals of Everlow. About a lion that would be bigger than a mare and unite the animals of the world to take back the land," declared Iza in a rough and deep voice as he looked at the guardian of the lion, Vera the cheetah.

The female cheetah stared into Iza's blue eyes for a long time. It was peculiar to see the old cat of the mountains come and choose her. Iza remained closest to the Burning Bush and understood what needed to be done. He was called the Priest of Pride, the founder of all knowledge and the one who would find Lion Ascend.

Vera looked at the mountain lion's white fur and long tail. The cheetah felt the cougar's energy embrace her body and realized that Iza was not here to make things difficult. Iza was like a mentor that all cats admired.

"It has been a long time since I heard the legend of the lion who will bring freedom to us all," said Vera. Her eyes panned down to the small cub nuzzling up against her paw that resembled a lion. The cheetah was already mother to three recently born cubs. How would she be able to raise a lion that would grow up to be the size of a stallion? She thought.

"Will you take Lion Ascend as your own?" asked Iza. "I beseech you Priest of Pride. I'm scared that I will fail you! I fear Voltar will send the wild dogs to destroy my family! Iza, take the cub to the mountains and raise him yourself, I beg you!" "Fear not Vera! You have been chosen by the Burning Bush. General Abel will watch over you," answered the Priest of Pride as he turned his head to the white wolf.

The white wolf stepped out from the shadows and looked at Vera. The Priest of Pride turned his head to look as Vera looked back at Abel with a nod. "He is willing to fulfill the commitment needed for this cub because he is strong, faithful and bold." "In the days I see before me, I feel I will stand in darkness. How will I know what to do?" asked Vera.

"Do only what you must, keep Lion Ascend safe from the empire of the tigers. My friends will watch over and keep you safe," assured Iza, as they both looked upon the helpless baby that began to cry. Vera's ears perked up to the sound of the cries and felt pity for the lion that had no mother or father. "I will do as you wish," replied Vera, as she bowed her head gracefully. She watched Iza smile as he nodded and looked at her. Suddenly, a shooting star flew through the heavens and Iza turned to Vera and Lion Ascend.

"Look, a shooting star, Vera! It's a promise to the cats and all animals from the Burning Bush that we will be saved! It's been predicted for thousands of years that Lion Ascend will lead us and become a magnificent leader to salvation. You will see it, I promise you!" declared Iza.

The star belonged to the night of the cheetah and the cub. Vera hoped it was a promise that they would be protected. The cheetah slowly smiled and felt excitement. After witnessing such a wonderful event; she wondered what would become of their future. Vera felt a new sense of hope that hadn't reached her dreams for many years.

Abel would have to be brave in order to protect Vera from Prince Voltar and the wild dogs. The white wolf let out a howl and immediately his sons and daughter joined in the howl that was louder than any group of howls before. The other wolves in Everlow and through out the land answered back, sometimes with multiple howls. It was the excitement of a recently born lion that would re-unite the land as it once was. Tears raised in Vera's eyes as she witnessed the sounds of howls returning to Abel. The wolves celebrated with excitement by dancing around, wrestling and then disappeared leaving their father, Iza and Vera alone.

She picked up the cub with her mouth and began the long walk from the mountains to Everlow Forest. The Priest of Pride watched the cheetah disappear from sight and turned to Abel who stood next to him. The Priest of Pride could tell there was something wrong from the worry in Abel's eyes.

"Voltar's strength grows stronger every day, my lord. The jackals and the hyenas grow in numbers. My scouts have determined that Prince Voltar has returned to help Tyrone kill Lion Ascend," warned General Abel.

"My children have revealed that we are being pushed to the south, to the desert. Cain keeps intercepting my sons who go hunting and demanding a ransom for Lion Ascend in order to hunt on the tiger's land," replied Abel.

"He will fail," began Iza. "Have faith Abel, the time has come for the return of the great lion," declared Iza as he turned his head to the white wolf.

Abel asked with concern, "What will you tell the Burning Bush?"

"I will tell the Burning Bush that everything is going as planned and the great

Lion has come to save us from evil!" said Iza as he stood up from sitting on the cold grass covered with dew. "We will have to wait until the cub has grown older, but until then watch over the cheetah and her family," he continued.

The mountain cat looked into Abel's blue eyes with an anxious look as though he knew his troubles. The white wolf took a deep breath to shake off the worries from such a bottled mind. Soon the world would be a better place for all the animals in the world and the prophecy would be complete. Abel was a general to the Priest of Pride; other than protecting Everlow and his own family he now had the added responsibility to protect the family of cheetahs.

"I must take my leave Abel. Watch over them, care for them until Lion Ascend is ready for the training," commanded Iza as he walked towards the mountains.

"I will," answered the white wolf. The elder began walking to the entrance of a cave to rest and clear his mind. There inside the cave he would begin setting up the training for Lion Ascend.

Abel watched his friend disappear in the distance and listened to the sound of flapping wings in the tree.

"The night is young General Abel for the death of a lion."

"What do you want Jezebel?" demanded the white wolf as he stared at the black crow with glowing red eyes. Jezebel opened up his wings and glided down to Abel with an evil sneer upon his twisted beak. Abel began to growl and revealed his shiny white teeth.

"I understand you are protecting a young cub," cracked Jezebel.

"I don't serve you, crooked bird. If you get in my way, I will rip you apart!" growled Abel.

"The hour grows late for the death of the lion cub. You will see his dead hide before you," Jezebel snarled.

"Never!" exclaimed the wolf.

"We shall see," laughed the twisted crow as he took flight through the air leaving the white wolf upset. Abel embraced the night and walked to his den to plan for the survival of Lion Ascend.

The sun rose from the east and heated the land. Vera stepped outside the den and looked around. She hoped it was safe to let her cubs play today, but kept in mind that after a year of protection, Lion Ascend would be taken to Iza.

After weeks of restricting the children to the den she decided to let them out. Vera watched the cubs play together and could see Lion Ascend was different.

Near Everlow Forest and upon the bluff of rock sat Abel with twenty of his kinsmen. He watched the cubs play in the grass from the bluff as a huge eagle named Enoch, swooped down next to him. The white wolf watched the four children wander away from the den and turned to Enoch.

"What have you seen with your great eyes?" he asked.

"Jezebel is near the cubs and our enemy Cain is outside of Everlow Forest with a small contingent. They will reach the den by nightfall."

"Follow Jezebel and report back any new information," answered Abel.

The honorable wolves waited for the chance to serve the future king Lion Ascend and were eager to begin the march. Sampson, the oldest with a red fur coat looked into his father's eyes and waited for orders to start the battle with Cain. Avian the black and white wolf waited next to Sampson as did Adias who was pure black. Knightly the speckled grey and white wolf had just trotted to meet with his father as did their sister Kayda who was a white wolf with black on the ends of her fur. They were the captains of their own group of wolves.

"Father, what are your orders?" asked Sampson.

"Assemble the rest of the pack!" ordered Abel.

The male cheetahs were curious as to why their brother had no spots on his body. They called Lion Ascend LA for short because he had such a long name. Vera followed her cubs when they wandered away to watch them play.

The cubs wrestled around in the shade of the forest; the tall grass provided comfort to lie down and wrestle. The birds chirped and the wind continued to blow as the day unfolded. It was mid-day, the cubs let out a light roar as they continued to bite, chew and kick each other for dominants. All three of the cheetah cubs did not have the strength to take on LA, but it was all fun and games for the baby lion. Vera knew the children's wrestling match had gone too far when she heard a light cry from Nikkita and ran over to witness what was going on. LA had swung his paw and sent Nikkita rolling backwards inside of a log, which was followed with the sound of a loud thud.

Lion Ascend felt a sharp feeling of guilt stretch across his shoulders that Nikkita might be hurt and trotted over to see how she was. Except before he reached the opening of the log, Chalice and Lobby jumped down on the cub from the top of the timber.

"Ouch," roared the lion as he rolled along the ground with the two cheetahs biting and clawing with the kick of their hind legs. Nikkita scuttled out of the log and grabbed hold of the back of her brother's neck. The lion cub cocked his head down like a bull and ran backwards to a sharp stop. LA raised and thrust his head down and as he shook his body like a dog he felt his siblings lose their grip. The lion then ran around in a small circle until his captors lost their grip and fell off. LA turned his head and watched them sail through the air and somersault through the grass. They got up slowly and looked grimly at LA.

"Come on LA you can at least let us beat you for once!" exclaimed Chalice.

"I'm sorry, as I understand it, there's three of you and only me," laughed Lion Ascend.

"But you've beaten us every time we play this game and its getting on my nerves!" declared Lobby.

"Well, what are you going to do? I obviously can wrestle all three of you at once!"

The three cheetahs looked at each other and then charged after the lion with all
their might. Lion Ascend continued to laugh with excitement as they wrestled him to the ground. Suddenly he saw a big, black shadow of a large bird. It landed in the trees, turned its head at the cubs and opened its beak to let out a shriek. LA could see the red eyes of the bird stare into his and felt his blood begin turning into ice.

"Guys stop! There's something watching us from the trees!" exclaimed Lion Ascend.

"Where?" asked Nikkita as she looked around into the bark and leaves, but she could not find the beast. The cubs stopped in their wrestling match to see what he was talking about.

Chalice's yellow eyes grew wide very quickly at the sight of the creature spreading its wings as though it were preparing to attack. It blended well in the darkness of the leaves and branches with only its red eyes staring back at them. Lion Ascend could feel the goose bumps rise in his beautiful, thick, golden fur. The wicked bird squawked and hissed at the cubs that slowly moved back. Nikkita looked around to find a place to hide and saw the hollow log that was behind them. As quick as lightning the three cats followed Nikkita to the hollow shaft just as the crow took flight. The crooked bird crowed and squawked at the cubs as it tried to get inside the dead remains of the tree, but realized there was no way to get in without Lion Ascend swiping him with his claws.

The lion hissed each time the crow lunged its beak and sharp talons in an effort to grip the lion's fur. The crow renounced itself from the log to see all four cats glaring and hissing at the bird to go away. The beast was not going to give up its will to kill the lion and proceeded back into the log. "Come out and play children." Screeched the crooked bird as he began laughing, "And wrestle with Uncle Jezebel."

"You're not our uncle," yelled Chalice.

"Don't talk to him," hushed Nikkita.

"We don't talk to strangers," replied Lobby.

"Yea and there's nothing stranger than a bird wanting to play with cats," said Chalice.

"Oh come now! Just give me a chance to get close to you," replied the crow as he lunged his beak at Lion Ascend, who was protecting his siblings.

"No! Get out!" shouted the cats together.

Suddenly, something grabbed the bird quickly with its mouth and paws, which left black feathers scattered around the ground. It was Vera, the mother, sworn to protect the cub as well as her own children. Lion Ascend's mouth dropped as he and the other cubs walked out of the log to watch their mother stand between the log and the offender that dared to attack the four innocent cubs.

"Leave me and my children!" demanded Vera as she stood ready to jump up at the crow.

"Give me the lion!" demanded the crow as he squint his red eyes at the mother cheetah.

Vera caught her breath from the powerful strike of the fight, "if you return I will kill you!" she threatened.

"I will be back, foolish cheetah," replied the crow as he lifted to the air, "and you will be killed."

Mother cheetah took a deep breath while turning around to face the log that was hiding the cubs. They slowly crept out more, realizing that she had won the fight with the crow. They crowded together nudging Vera's warm heart with kisses and playful nudges from their paws. Vera realized that it wasn't over; an evil entity was working against them to make things difficult.

Vera walked back to the den with the children in front of her. There was nothing in sight except the children wrestling with each other, but it was obvious that their games were growing more aggressive. She watched Lion Ascend wrestle with the cubs and noticed how much stronger he was. Mother cheetah knew something tragic was going to happen if he continued to grow and become stronger. He would possibly injure them while playing around.

"Guys stop rough housing that evil bird could still come back," she commanded while smelling the air.

"Sorry, mother," they said together and continued to follow her after she passed them.

Vera felt there was hope in Lion Ascend to make things the way they once were and bring freedom for all the animals. The day would come when LA would stop Tyrone, Prince Voltar and King Estargo. The empire of the tigers controlled the animals from hunting to traveling.

Tyrone was one of the most feared tigers throughout the land. He was second in command to Prince Voltar. Tyrone controlled the region of Everlow and was trying to gain support by using fear to get control of all the animals.

It was clear that Tyrone was responsible for the death of a lot of cheetahs and leopards including her mate Rythemic. The battle began with the attack of Tyrone's army marching from the north. It was the last time she spoke to Rythemic before he died. A tear emerged from Vera's eyes, as she smelled lilacs, they served in her memory of grieving. She prayed that Rythemic wouldn't die in vain and that the prediction would follow true. The beautiful thoughts of Lion Ascend persisted while Vera listened to the cubs talk to each other.

Enoch swooped down to the tree and folded his wings to watch over the family. As the day unfolded the cubs were able to play close to the den in view of Vera. Enoch watched from the lowest branch to see Vera take care of Lion Ascend. It was a time of innocence and he enjoyed watching the cubs play together. He smiled and laughed as the lion and the cheetahs pounced on each other.

The eagle turned his head to the sky as he heard the calls from the hawks to the crows in the distance. Enoch spread his wings and took to the sky. He had a feeling that Jezebel was near and knew that he was the only bird in the area that could keep up. Enoch spread his wings to harness the wind and flew through the air as fast as he could.

He flew higher and higher until he was rushing through the clouds. The large bird looked below to see the black crow flying slowly below him. The sun unleashed its stimulating heat upon the great bird and would blind Jezebel from seeing him. Enoch felt the wind against his face and felt a drift of coldness stretch from his insides to both tips of his wings. The sound of thunder could be heard as the beginning of a storm from the north emerged. Enoch looked ahead to see volcanoes below him and kept his eyes on Jezebel.

They passed though the mountain range and volcanoes known as the Bad Lands. The volcanoes were spitting out magma as they had for hundreds of years. The Bad Lands was a place that the tigers and other animals of evil lived after it had been abandoned by the lions.

Enoch flew through smoke and lost sight of Jezebel, but the shadows of the volcanoes could be seen. The eagle flew closer to the black volcanoes and felt the hot levels of hell spill near him. He remembered the stories told long ago that the volcanoes never used to exist and that the land used to be a meadow. The Bad Lands didn't emerge until the lions were eliminated. Flash backs emerged in Enoch's mind of the past battles that were lost to the tigers that took place on the Bad Lands.

The eagle reached a dead volcano called Death Mountain

and watched the crow fly through the top of it. Enoch landed on the side of the volcano near an opening that led inside and cautiously walked in. He walked around on the ledge and realized that he was high in the roof of the volcano. The great bird looked around to see big birds just below him as well as hundreds of tigers, hyenas, coyotes and jackals talking amongst themselves.

Enoch could hear one of them talk about a grand march to destroy the wolves and the lion cub. A tiger that sat in the throne rose up from the shadows and stepped near the pond of magma that gave light. Enoch heard the other tigers call him Lord Tyrone and bowed to him. All the tigers respected him with the nod of their heads.

"My brothers and sisters soon we shall have revenge and rip the hearts out of the last believers!" boasted Tyrone.

"General Cabass tell our followers what our plans are," ordered Tyrone as he turned his head to the tiger emerging from the dark.

"We shall destroy the prophecy of Lion Ascend," declared General Cabass as Tyrone nodded his head.

"We shall kill the lion and crush the wolves who dare to resist us as the new rulers of Ayana. We shall see the end of Lion Ascend and kill the cheetah that protects him!" continued General Cabass. There was a huge cheer from all the animals as they all chanted, "kill Lion Ascend!"

They all became silent as a visitor that the tigers feared most, emerged from the shadows. He was twice the size of Tyrone and would be described by many of the tigers as rigid, dictorial, arrogant and evil. The tiger was well known throughout the land and had conquered a rebellion several miles north of the Bad Lands. When Prince Voltar received word that Lion Ascend was born he wanted to meet with Tyrone immediately. The big tiger made his way to Tyrone and with each step of the way, the tigers looked intimidated.

"Prince Voltar, we're honored by your presence," said Tyrone.

With his deep rough voice he replied, "I've received word from King Estargo that you have found Lion Ascend. The one sworn by the prophecy, to destroy our empire! Why do you delay the attack?"

"Yes my lord," began Tyrone. "I must say, would it be honorable to kill the lion when he's grown up?"

"Silence!" snarled Voltar as he walked around Tyrone in a circle. "You've wasted so much time on the search and destroy order that I wish to kill you now," hissed Voltar.

"Sir, you forget that the king has appointed me lordship of this area, not you!" answered Tyrone

"That was a mistake! You're weak Tyrone! If you do not act now, you will regret not killing the lion. That lion is destined to unite all the animals in the world against us, not just the cats," declared Voltar.

"Step aside my lord! Everlow is mine! My forces shall kill the small rebellion of wolves and we shall kill the Priest of Pride. Does that not satisfy you?" demanded Tyrone.

"For the moment," answered Voltar. "I'm going to be leaving now, but I shall return. When I do, I better see a dead lion!"

Enoch heard enough and turned around to escape, just as a piece of rock got kicked by his foot from the ledge. The pebble fell on a flock of crows and toppled down near Tyrone's foot. There was a stir of noises as they looked around and saw the eagle. The birds made way towards him like a deadly swarm of bees. Enoch gasped in fright as he watched the birds fly towards him and took flight to the air.

"Find the intruder and kill him!" exclaimed Tyrone as he let out a snarl, followed by a line of growls and howls from the hundreds of followers.

The golden eagle flew higher and higher to escape the pursuits of the enemy. Enoch thrusted his wings hard against the dark clouds and could see nothing, but the shadows of fire stirring from the volcanoes. The great bird turned his head to see the large group of hawks, crows and ravens flying after him in a swarm of shadows behind the smoke. The eagle began to get tired and his lungs began to feel like they were on fire. The bird let out a cry to his friends in the distance. He cleared the smog and found himself above the mountains and in the distance was Everlow Forest waiting for his arrival.

Seconds turned to minutes, soon he saw Everlow forest and twenty eagles swarmed together to rescue him. Six albatrosses, giant thunderous birds of the east joined the eagles and glided with their wings spread apart to attack. The eagles and the hawks clawed and snipped at each other. It wasn't until the albatrosses drew near that the invaders realized the attack was hopeless. The albatrosses ate many of the hawks and with the power of their sharp talons they sent the remainder of the injured birds floundering in flight. Enoch let out a sigh of relief as he watched the enemy withdraw.

They had saved the day and were able to join Enoch after all was well.

Enoch glided through the air in grace, with twenty eagles flying beside him and six albatrosses hovering above them. The sun was shining brightly over head and pierced through the white clouds. In a single strike of brightness from the sun, the light shined intensely, leading the way to the wolves. Enoch looked near the bluffs and saw the wolves gather around, howling as well as barking, waiting for him to land. He swooped down to catch the pleasure of the pups as they barked in excitement. The golden eagle turned his head to smile at the teenage wolves that were happy to see him. Enoch flew back and stretched his wings as he slowly glided to the ground in front of General Abel and his sons.

"Tyrone plans to kill the lion tonight," warned Enoch.

"By what words would tigers dare to cross Everlow?" asked Knightly just as Abel turned his head in front of Knightly to signal for absolute silence.

"We shall make preparations for tonight," ordered General Abel. The sun shined overhead and the white wolf knew they would have to assemble by dusk. The day would be at a close, but the night would be the beginning to a new war.

Dusk came and the cubs continued to play and wrestle with each other. They played around another log that was closer to the den. Lobby scuttled through the opening until Lion Ascend pounced on him. "Ha, I got you!" laughed LA.

"That hurt brother!" cried Lobby.

"Well you better get use to it, I'm bigger than you," answered Lion Ascend.

"Lion Ascend! Stop what you're doing and have a good heart!" The words pierced the lion's ears as Vera ran over and kissed Lobby's head.

"Yea, have a good heart," repeated Nikkita with a smile.

"What does that mean, mother?" asked Lion Ascend as he watched his siblings run off and play.

Vera waited for the moment to teach a lesson in manners. "What it means is one day I will be gone and you will be left with only each other. Be kind to the loving beings around you. The big ones as well as the small, for they will come to you when you need them most." "Mother, I will never lose you," he replied.

"I hope, I never lose you," answered Vera with a smile.

Mother cheetah looked at her son and continued to glow with joy as she realized how special he was. Vera could feel her heart beat faster as thoughts raced through her head, knowing, if necessary that she would die for him. "One day you will be faced with the biggest fear of your life and you will no longer fear anything."

"Why?" asked Lion Ascend.

"Don't you want to be courageous?" laughed Vera.

"Well of course! I just don't know where to look," answered Lion Ascend.

"Courage isn't something you look for, it's a power within you," said Vera. Then she paused to her son who looked at her confused, "what's the matter?"

"I'm not courageous," he answered sadly.

"You will find your courage and be able to help others,"

she declared and watched a smile emerge on his face.

"Really," he replied as he nuzzled his head into hers.

"You will become so courageous that you'll come to my rescue when I'm in trouble, now go play."

As Lion Ascend turned to join the cubs, Vera realized something strong had taken place. He was young and innocent but the day would come when he would find his courage. "Lion Ascend, I would die for you," she whispered while watching him run in the distance to tackle Chalice. Vera could feel the numbness strike her back as she heard the tiny little roars from the lion. It was weak and high pitched, but soon it would embrace itself into a very deep roar that would shake the land. She imagined Lion Ascend as the mighty lion that the prophecy foretold. He would become great in size with a thunderous roar and strength to uphold love, truth and honesty.

The day drew to a close as the sun hid behind the trees. The blue sky began to turn dark purple with dashes of red and yellow from the sunset. Vera watched the cubs wrestle with each other and listened to the voice in her head about Lion Ascend meeting with Iza. The Priest of Pride would meet Lion Ascend and begin the training that would transform him into a warrior. The darkness filled the forest and unleashed its fear upon the good creatures that lived there. One day the tigers would give up the stolen land and disband their army from the great lion of the ascending realm.

Abruptly, the cheetah felt the light vibrations along the ground from the wild dogs of animals that she presumed was sent by Lord Cain. Her ears heard the sound of running and her eyes spotted a flock of sparrows leaving. She sniffed the air and tasted the essence of jackals as well as coyotes. Her ears perked up after hearing the footsteps and the sound of reckless dogs' panting.

"Get inside the den now!" ordered Vera as her eyes watched the rabbits run away, warning her of the danger that was coming. The cubs ran past her with the light sound of their feet scuffing the grass. Mother cheetah looked up to the damaging sky and watched as the storm clouds rumbled in folds upon each other.

Wind rustled the trees and blew through the tall grass, another warning for her to protect the lion. Then an eagle flew down and landed near the cheetah. Its golden feathers stretched upward in the air and its head turned to Vera.

"Who are you and what do you want?" demanded Vera as she was about to pounce on the large bird.

"I'm Enoch! I was sent by General Abel to warn you that Cain and the wild dogs are coming to kill you!"

"This is my home and I will die to protect my children," replied Vera.

Enoch saw the courage in her eyes and hoped that it would be enough to fight them off. "Very well, I will try to help you," he said. He flew to the lowest branch of the nearest tree and prayed that General Abel would make it to the den in time.

Vera walked over to the entrance of the den; smelled the air and looked around
for danger but found none. As night set in, Vera watched the shadows behind the trees grow big and scary. The brush of the wind rode the grass as she swung her tail back and forth while thinking for answers to her intuitions. Small drops of rain fell upon her face and the sound of thunder cascaded through her ears. The rain fell thick upon her and quickly the cheetah stepped inside the den to guard the entrance.

Minutes seemed to pass like hours until something crept towards the entrance of the den. The five dark figures walked towards the hole through the rain with no fear of who was protecting the lion. Within the darkness of the entrance, mother cheetah growled and let out a snarl from her soaked face. "Come any closer and I will rip you to shreds!"    "We're on special orders," said the leader who was a coyote.

Mother cheetah crept out slowly and felt the sprinkles of rain. The moon was glowing and left the trees, as well as the grass, blue with black shadows. Vera knew the coyotes and jackals were interested in killing Lion Ascend. As the clouds veiled the moon, she could see the blue begin to fade away and darkness took over.

"My name is Talick, we know you have the lion," replied

Talick.

Vera cried, "I don't care who you are! I won't let you in!"

Unexpectedly there was a howl, Vera could hear the cry and it sent shivers up spine. She watched Talick's ears perk up as well as his eyes open wide in surprise. Twenty wolves surrounded the wild dogs and stared at the creatures.

"I have nothing to show you," Vera growled.

"Maybe you should leave Talick! You're out numbered," protested General Abel.

Talick looked up at General Abel who licked his lips and began to growl. "I shall leave, but I'll be back."

The white wolf heard the howls in the distance and knew that there was going to be more than enough wolves to take on the enemy's army. "I'm going to count to ten. If you're still here; we're going to attack," growled General Abel.

As the count down progressed, three of the dogs were intimidated by the threat and left, leaving only two wild dogs. The moon unveiled itself to light up the area and revealed all the wolves that had gathered to protect Vera's area. Talick felt his veins turn to ice and felt death enter his body as the white wolf's blue eyes glared at him. General Abel got to six before Talick and his associates rose up and turned to retreat.

"We'll be back! When we do, Cain will be here with about fifty of us! We'll see how well you can handle us then," said Talick.

The white wolf ceased his count down and watched the wild dogs run away. The air was cool, with sprinkles of rain falling on his face. He was burdened with worry about the future. Abel looked at his sons and daughter and felt the presence of doubt in their eyes. The white wolf looked up at the full moon and then to Vera who looked at him with comforting eyes.

General Abel saved the day so that she and the cubs could live. The night was young and Vera was looking forward to sleeping in peace. A night of peace well earned.

Scene 5
1,561

The two dogs left and would not be back tonight. General

Abel walked over to the
entrance and saw Vera curled up with the cubs. She looked into the
white wolf's eyes and knew that it wasn't over. "They will be
back, and in greater numbers," said General Abel. The white wolf
turned around to talk to Sampson about the next course of action
and left Vera alone with the cubs.

Vera extinguished the last bit of fear that remained with her
since the wild dogs had appeared. They would have to fight for
Everlow and for her right to remain in the den. The question
emerged; how did they know where she was? Then the haunting
thought of Jezebel trying to kill the cubs emerged in such mind.
The wild dogs were not from this region, but they would be back to
slaughter them.

The night came to pass, the owls and birds watched over
the den to be sure the wild dogs did not return. Mother cheetah
kept the cubs warm and listened for any intruders that would draw
near. For as long as the sun would shine and the moon remained lit
she would die to protect them. She heard the sound of wolves
walking around the entrance and then felt safe. Her eyes slowly
opened as Abel and Enoch stepped inside her home.

"You've been discovered by our enemy," began Abel.

"This is my home!" she replied.

"If you want to protect your children then you must leave
tonight," ordered the white wolf as he got up and left the den.

The light sprinkles of rain fell upon his face as Abel gave
orders to his sons. Their plan was to build a perimeter against an
attack, for General Abel had a feeling there would be another
attack soon.

"We must keep the boundary free from invasion," ordered
General Abel to his sons and daughter. "Enoch, I want you to
assemble the eagles and albatrosses!" he ordered.

With the mighty number of wolves behind General Abel's
command he was preparing for the worst. The rain ceased and he
closed his eyes to pray that he would receive a glimmer of hope.
After patrolling and receiving reports from his sons, he lay near the
den to rest.

Abel opened his eyes after hearing footsteps and turned his head to his son Avian. The white wolf looked at his black and white son and knew what Avian was going to say. "Father, we've got a problem at the eastern edge of the forest."

"What is it?" asked the general, expecting bad news.

"The enemy is marching here."

"Where are Sampson, Knightly and Adias?" asked Abel.

"They left with seventeen others to meet them head on."

"What!" growled General Abel.

Suddenly, the sprinkles turned into heavy rain, as thunder rumbled through the clouds. Avian and his father looked up to the sky and felt the drops of water pelt their body. It seemed that this weather was going to torment them through battle as well.

Vera's ears perked up while cleaning her fur coat and she quickly exited the den. She was listening to the general's conversation and was worried that they would be leaving her. She could feel her heart begin to thump and hear the continued cries by the wolves. She ran to the general, "what's going on? Why are the wolves howling against the star lit sky? Where are you going?"

"Get back inside and be prepared to leave the den with the children. A blood battle is expected and I don't know if we'll win!" exclaimed Abel as he left Vera and joined the pack.

Lion Ascend poked his head out from the entrance of the den and was surprised. He had never seen so many wolves near the den. What was going on and where were they all going? he thought

"Mother what's going on?" asked Lion Ascend.

"Get back inside!" she ordered as the strikes of wind cried in screams against her ears and the sprinkles of rain persisted upon her face, hiding such tears from the cubs.

The moon was unveiled by the clouds and shined down upon the meadow that was between the forest and the mountains. Twenty feet away stood fifty dark figures. Their eyes were glowing yellow and orange as though fallens possessed them. The white wolf trotted out from the brush after Avian and Kayda to find Sampson leading a large number of wolves.

The leader of the wild dogs was a hyena named Cain who trotted to the middle of the field, leaving his band of hyenas, coyotes and jackals behind. Cain, the leader of the wild dogs took his orders from General Cabass and Tyrone. Cain knew General Abel by reputation and was confident to win a battle against the white wolf.

Sampson and Knightly galloped to meet them as well. General Abel, Avian and Kayda joined them in the middle of the field. Both groups could feel the rain hit their face and the thunder of the heavens ring in their ears. General Abel knew Cain by reputation as well and heard that he was a very strong ferocious fighter.

The large hyena looked at Sampson then to Abel with a sneer. Cain was twice the size of Abel and therefore was very intimidating. The general licked his lips and waited for Cain to speak.

"The night is young my brother. Why don't you step aside and let us enter?" asked Cain.

"If you try to get through, I shall rip you apart!" growled Sampson.

"You have a brave boy General Abel, but is he prepared to die tonight?" growled Cain. Abel ignored the question, "I can't allow you to pass on our territory. These are sacred grounds to the wolves and the Burning Bush."

"I don't believe you realize that these lands belong to Tyrone and Prince Voltar," answered Cain.

"No wolf of Everlow shall submit to your rule. There are over fifty wolves here, an equal match to your band. Disband and go home," ordered General Abel as he turned his head to see something walking towards them.

In the distance, a figure was walking in the middle of the two rivalries, it was the Priest of Pride. The white wolf was relieved and knew that if there was anything that could be done it was Iza who could create a solution. As miraculous as it was, it had stopped raining and only the water dripping from their furs could be seen.

Cain turned to the ghostly cat and began to growl, "what do you want?"

"I want peace," answered Iza.

"Peace is for the weak!" exclaimed Talick.

"Don't you find killing a baby lion unchallenging?" asked the Priest of Pride.

"It's not my decision to make," replied Cain.

"The prophecy foretells the coming of a great war between good and evil. Don't you believe that it would be best to let the cub grow up before you kill him?"

"Maybe," answered Cain.

"Well there now, we have something that would help us decide the fate of the cub," cracked Iza.

"I have my orders, the cub must die!" demanded Cain

Iza needed to deter Cain somehow, "there is no honor in killing a baby lion."

"I don't want him trained," answered Cain.

"Very well, can you at least wait a year before invading the forest? That would make you look honorable," Iza said hoping to buy them more time to train Lion Ascend.

"Yes, I can do that." Then, Cain realized what he had agreed to and stammered, "I mean, wait a minute. Who are you to say what I can do!"

"Now, now, you did say yes. So by the laws of Prince Voltar you will have to wait one year before entering Everlow," smiled Iza.

Cain turned around to disband the army. The wolves smiled and watched the wild dogs gallop away in the distance. The white wolf looked at the Priest of Pride with a sigh of relief. If it wasn't for Iza they surely would have fought.

"What took you so long?" asked Abel.

"You may still need to guard the forest. I was able to talk the wild dogs into a peaceful hypnotized solution, but it remains to be seen if they will follow it," answered Iza.

Abel trotted with his band of wolves to the cheetah's home. Vera was cuddled with her children in fear that it would be their last night together. General Abel was happy that the Priest of Pride had brought them more time to prepare for the inevitable battle that would take place in a year. "Vera, everything is ok," said the white wolf with comfort.

Vera stepped outside to see Abel and knew that they would be able to sleep without any worries until morning. Lion Ascend would be given a chance to live and grow up to face his destiny. It would take time before the cub would understand that his need was imperative. Together as a family they slept without fear; Vera opened her eyes with a terrible thought that their future was scheduled for war and there was nothing she could do to prevent it.

*Nikkita opened her eyes and saw clouds floating around her. The sky was blue with stars of every size. She jumped from one cloud to the next. The cheetah landed on a cloud and looked down from it to see the wonderful glow of evergreens. It was the forest below with the most beautiful stream ever seen. With one step off the cloud she found herself on the grass.*

*She looked around to see how perfectly content the trees were. The rich smell of lilacs filled her with excitement. The sound of a stream could be heard just ahead. Nikkita could feel the wet dew dampen her paws, but she didn't care and continued to walk around. The cheetah walked through the forest and beautiful flowers to see the stream. Her eyes opened with amazement to the sight of Lion Ascend, he was still a cub, and hadn't earned his mane yet. He kneeled down to take a drink of water.*

*"LA, what are you doing here?" asked Nikkita.*

*"I'm enjoying myself in Heaven. How about you?" he answered.*

*"I've come to tell you that I love you"*

*"I love you to sister."*

*"No you don't understand, we're not bonded that*

*way," replied Nikkita.*    *"Really!" said Lion*
*Ascend.*

  *"Yes," cried Nikkita.*
  *"What would mother say?" asked Lion Ascend.*
  *"Mother would say the same. You're as bright as a*
*star and we don't have to live apart!"*
  *Suddenly, she felt the splash of water hit her face.*
*There was a burst of laughter unleashed from Lion Ascend*
*as he trotted away from her. "You're going to get it,"*
*gasped Nikkita as she wrestled him to the ground. They*
*wrestled and played for as long as time would allow them.*
  *"Nikkita," yelled a feminine voice.*
  *"What?" Nikkita asked*
  *"Are you going to help Chalice and Lobby with the*
*hunt?"*
  *"What?" The cheetah asked as she looked around.*

"Nikkita!—"

"What!" she replied while opening her eyes and realized
the beautiful moment was only a dream. She raised herself from
the ground to stretch her back and felt it crack.

  "Check on your brothers to make sure they're ok," ordered
Vera.

  Nikkita walked out of the new den, in the mountains near
the wolves. She looked around to see Lobby and Chalice eating
what they hunted together. She stepped down the rocky floor to
get closer to her brothers. They were a year old and capable of
hunting there own game.

  "Where's Lion Ascend?" asked Nikkita.

  "He's out by the bluffs" answered Chalice.

Nikkita took off in a trot in the direction of the cliff overlooking
Everlow Forest. She jumped over logs, ran through a pond and
climbed up rugged rock until she finally got there. She saw him
looking away with his back turned

  "Lion Ascend are you ok? Mother has been worried," lied
Nikkita. She slowly walked closer, looking at the thick golden

mane that had grown thicker around his neck over the last few months. Nikkita loved the way he looked with the golden mane because she thought he looked amazing.

He turned around, slowly looking sad, "I look and feel hideous."

"You're not ugly," answered Nikkita as she walked closer to him.

"Yes I am, I don't have spots like you or your incredible speed."

"You're amazing," replied Nikkita as she smiled. "Don't let anyone tell you different."

Lion Ascend turned around to face the sun and wondered what he was doing here. It was mid-morning and the lion wasn't happy with the changes that he was seeing. Where were the lions? Where did he come from? Nikkita rubbed up against his right shoulder to ease his pain. "I care about you," she said with comfort in her eyes.

Her eyes looked into his as he looked uneasy. He looked away, to the direction of the sun, hoping to get answers to such questions. Nikkita was his sister and having feelings for her was an uncharted area for him.

"Nikkita, I don't feel it should be in my nature to be a part of you."

"You're already a part of me. You have feelings for me, I've felt it. Don't push     me away."

"What about our mother? How is she going to feel about us?"

"Who cares, she knows that you're not my brother and so does Chalice and Lobby," she answered.

The sound of a twig cracked and he turned around to see that it was his two brothers. They looked confused at big brother when they saw their sister with him. Nikkita looked sad, but tried to hide it by smiling. Before they were able to speak, a scream was heard. It was what Lion Ascend needed to avoid questions that he didn't want to answer.

"Come!" commanded Lion Ascend and his brothers

followed.

Nikkita walked slowly through the forest, with a feeling of sadness, left behind by the one she loved. The cheetah wondered what had gone wrong and wondered if she would reach his heart. She walked with her head faced down and could see it was getting darker in the forest. When she raised her head she saw small orbs of light that lit up near a tree. Hundreds of white stars began flying around in circles until they formed into a peculiar figure.

She had the face of a monkey, stood upwards on two legs and wore a dress made of sliver leaves. Nikkita could see that this person had no fur on her upper body. The figure was flying and spread her white wings in the air like a bird. Smaller size orbs began falling down and others flew around her while glowing with a silver color.

"There now," the figure said softly as she glided down while stepping her strange six digit feet to the ground and kneeled down.

"Who are you?" asked Nikkita while stepping away.

"Don't be afraid. My name is Dafidale and I live here in the woods with the Xeras. I heard you crying and you look like you need a friendly ear," smiled Dafidale.

Nikkita wiped her eyes with her paw and tried to hide such feelings from the stranger. "You couldn't possibly help me with the problem I have," answered Nikkita.

The Xera giggled, "I don't know, you haven't told me."

"The problem is I haven't seen another cheetah for quite some time and I've fallen in love with another cat."

"Well what's wrong with that?" asked the Xera

"He's my brother and for him it doesn't seem right."

"You're a cheetah and he's a cheetah?" asked Dafidale.

"Actually he's a lion," sobbed Nikkita.

"A lion! I haven't seen a lion for hundreds of years. The best advice I can give you is to have patience and follow your heart. He'll come for you and I have the perfect song to sooth your pain."

# Lion Ascend

Nikkita sat down and listened to the Xera sing. It was like the sound of robins and sparrows chirping during the morning breeze. Each syllable of the words unleashed a powerful feeling of healing in Nikkita's heart.

*there are things that can not be denied*
*in places that leave you at a halt*
*it seems that things can not remain*
*there are places that you will hide*
*in ways that have gone and died*

*there are ideas that can not lie*
*in spaces that abandon us in a vault*
*it seems that things are not in stain*
*there are places that we can hide*
*in ways that will never die*

*let me catch you when you fall*
*when you ever feel you're in doubt*
*when ever you're feeling despair*
*and you don't understand why*
*let me catch you when you fall*
*when you can feel that, I'm proud*
*things can always be repaired*

A smile emerged on Nikkita's face and she felt healed from such emotional pain. The Xera raised herself up from the ground and was much taller than expected. "You're beautiful," smiled Nikkita as she stood up from sitting. "How did you learn to sing like that?"

"I learned it many years ago when lions ruled the world. Tell the lion that the fulfillment of the prophecy awaits him," answered Dafidale

Nikkita had to see her again in the future and meet the other Xeras. "Dafidale is it ok to bring my brothers here including the one I love?"

"You can bring whoever you deem worthy, my dear," replied Dafidale.

Unexpectedly, Nikkita heard Lion Ascend calling her name. "I've got to go," she answered. "Take care and good luck with the lion," smiled the Xera. Nikkita ran through the dark woods until she got to the top. Lion Ascend was standing there waiting for her.

"Sorry, I needed to be alone," said Nikkita.

"Is everything ok?" he asked.

Nikkita turned her head to the forest then back to LA. She wanted to tell him about the new friend she made, but that would rest for another day. The cheetah turned her head back to the lion and nodded with a grin.

"Yes, everything is great."

"We managed to spook a coyote away from a baby deer and killed it. Lion Ascend led the way home and Nikkita followed him with a positive outlook for the future.

Lion Ascend spent the afternoon lying on the grass with his eyes closed. He was relaxed and could feel the sun's heat massage his back. The sound of birds chirped in the woods and the crickets played their violins within the shadows of the trees. It seemed everything was at peace and Lion Ascend let his mind wander away from Everlow. It wandered away from the forest, the mountains and soon the world.

*It was near dusk and the high pitch sound of the wind brushed up against his ear. Lion Ascend opened his eyes to see it was Nikkita. He raised himself from the ground and yawned.*

*"What's the matter?" he asked with a stare in her eyes.*

*"LA, I can't stop this feeling any longer!" Nikkita ran up to the lion and kissed him.*

*Lion Ascend raised his eyebrows in surprise for he had not experienced this before. The old friendship he treasured since he was young was being replaced with a* relationship that was unexplored. Now that he was older was it ok to have these feelings? Surely Nikkita would be better suited for another cheetah, but it was obvious she was in love with him.

"Forgive me! I've only meant to please you," replied Nikkita as she turned her head away.

"There's nothing to forgive. I'm the last of my kind and I want you," LA said shyly.

"I need you, now!" interrupted Nikkita.

"I'm your brother!" Once again Nikkita interrupted, "no you're not! You're a lion and the prophecy foretells you saving all of your brothers and sisters of the world. You weren't born of our mother's blood so therefore it is not

a sin to love me!" cried Nikkita as she panned and leaned her head up against his shoulder.

Lion Ascend looked into Nikkita's eyes. How could he refuse her affection when she needed him most? The spotted cat looked into his eyes and was so innocent and vulnerable to being hurt. The big lion leaned down to the cheetah's lips and kissed her. After all was well, Nikkita looked at him and smiled.

Suddenly, the wind took shape and blew through the leaves as a dangerous figure stood before the great lion. It was shaped like a tiger and flickered fire from its body. It had the symbol of annihilation and there seemed to be no way to destroy it. Its voice was rough and the lion could only imagine that it could turn lakes into blood and burn forests into deserts. "I've come to kill the lion just as I've killed the others!" said the beast.

Lion Ascend looked at the creature and was scared of what was in store for him. The feeling of lightning ran down his spine all the way to the tip of his tail. The creature stared at him with its dark eyes as it waited for Lion Ascend to attack.

*"Who are you?" demanded Lion Ascend.*

*"I am Death, Lord of air, thought, war and destruction. You shall die today as your ancestors have!"*

*The thought of all of the lions being struck down by this creature made him angry. The last assembly of the lions was gone because of the tigers. Now it made sense that the leader of the tigers was Death.*

*"I will not be your next victim!"*

*"Then is that a challenge foolish lion," roared the flaming tiger.*

*"LA, don't! I don't want to lose you?" replied Nikkita.*

*"Step aside, I've got to face Death," growled Lion Ascend.*

*Death began to bellow with laughter as he charged forward and swiped his claws across Lion Ascend's face. The lion could feel its burning, stinging sensation near his eyes. The scorching fire burned LA's back, stretching from his tail to his neck. "Lion Ascend!" cried Nikkita. "No, run Nikkita!" exclaimed Lion Ascend, as darkness slipped onto him. The wind screamed his name as the hour became late and then he realized he had been dreaming.*

The lion opened his eyes and gritted his teeth with great haste as he gasped for air. It was like a dark foreboding feeling of his heart ripping in two, which took his breath away. Lion Ascend rose from the ground and realized that the warmth of the sun hadn't left him. What did the dream mean? How could he come to terms of such actions or for falling in love with Nikkita? He was beginning to get a headache just thinking about it. Who was Death? The visit from the tiger would leave him wondering if he was going to die.

It seemed obvious that he needed to wake himself from this nightmare. Lion Ascend turned his head to see the small pond and thought how nice it would be to bathe
his troubles away. The lion ran to the crystal clear pond and dived

in, but didn't realize that he was being watched by Nikkita. Her golden eyes peered out from behind the tree.

The lion felt the warm water run against his mane and he could feel the bright sun hit his head. A humming bird flew around him to get his attention. The lion jumped out from the pool as the intense flutter annoyed him.

"Hello," asked Lion Ascend as he looked at the strange creature.

"Lion Ascend, I have a message to deliver."

"What's the message?"

"The Burning Bush wishes to meet with you, come now," replied the humming bird as it flew away in haste.

"Wait!" shouted Lion Ascend as he tried to keep up. The lion followed the humming bird through the woods and down a gully where roses, orchids, tulips and blueberry bushes grew. A small stream was in front of them and Lion Ascend felt his paws get wet as he kept up with the humming bird. He ran up the side of the culvert and braced a stump with his claws to pull himself up. He reached the end of the woods in an open meadow and saw something on fire. Lion Ascend stepped closer to see it was a small tree on fire, except it wasn't burning.

"We shall leave you alone my lord," said the humming bird.

Lion Ascend watched the humming bird disappear in the distance and turned his attention to the Burning Bush that stood before him with long flames of fire flickering in the air. Would this phenomenon be able to explain why things were? he wondered.

"Don't be afraid Lion Ascend. I will not harm you," the voice emanated from within the fire and bush. It was a feminine voice followed with a masculine voice that was speaking in perfect unison.

Lion Ascend was startled, "how do you know my name?"

"I know a lot about you. I created you to bring greatness in the free worlds. You're going to realize that you won't always have the answers, but in time you will understand what you need to do."

"What happened to the other lions?"

"The other lions have been killed by the tigers. It is up to you to free the lions that have been captured."

"How?" asked Nikkita.

"In time you will find them. After you're trained by Iza you shall be parted from the ones you love; the cheetah that took you in as her son, the brothers and sister you have grown to love on your journey are your companions. The white wolf, as well as the Priest of Pride will be parted from you and you must accept it."

"There must be something I can do to protect them!" cried Lion Ascend.

"There's nothing you can do to interfere with free will. What you can do is accept the training from Iza and unite the animals against evil."

"What if I fail?" Lion Ascend asked with mounting fear.

"You won't fail because I will be by your side. Go now and begin your training," said the Burning Bush.

Lion Ascend turned around to run back to the den. The answers to such questions weighed heavily over him. Would life be better after uniting the animals in harmony? Thought Lion Ascend. All of a sudden there was a voice whispering to him.

"If only you knew your true intention to this war." Lion Ascend turned to see it was a flower on fire.

"Who are you?" demanded the lion as he looked at the fire flower with the face of a tiger.

"I am Lord Slatan, the creator of Ayana. I command you to take your place with the tigers."

Lion Ascend was concerned because this creature had the face of a tiger, "why should I listen to a flower?"

"Why should you listen to the Burning Bush?" answered Lord Slatan

"I was guided to Him!"

"Wrong, you have been guided to me. The Burning Bush knows nothing of your kind. If you kneel down and sacrifice yourself to the tigers you shall save the animals of Everlow, especially your sister."

"You know nothing about me. My destiny is to have a good heart!" roared Lion Ascend as he beheaded the flower with his claws and left.

The sun still loomed overhead and he would have to return to the den and prepare for his meeting with the Priest of Pride tomorrow. Lion Ascend wondered what the day would bring. He was a lion; the last of his kind, yet he was living in peace with a family of cheetahs. His brothers looked up to him, the wolves protected him and Nikkita loved him. The Burning Bush warned him that he would be parted from those he loved. What did it mean? And who was Slatan? All these thoughts cluttered his mind.

Lion Ascend walked past his brothers who were wrestling with each other. Nikkita was lying in the sun relaxing and opened her eyes to see Lion Ascend standing in front of her. The two were silent and Lion Ascend looked uneasy.

"Is mother here?" he asked.

"She's sleeping in the den," answered Nikkita as she looked at him and could tell he was about to speak.

LA started to say, "I have something to tell you."

"I have something to tell you," interrupted Nikkita as she rose up.

Lion Ascend continued, "I was led to the Burning Bush."

Nikkita exclaimed, "The Burning Bush! Oh my God! Nobody, but the Priest of Pride has been able to visit the Burning Bush. It's a blessing Lion Ascend. Don't be afraid of what it has in store for you."

"The Burning Bush told me what I must do and I'm a little uneasy on how to proceed. I'm sorry for any heartache I caused you."

"Don't be silly," began Nikkita. "You were only doing what you thought was best."

"I do care about you, but there's so much at stake. I learned that not all the lions

have been killed," replied Lion Ascend.

"Are you sure?" she asked.

"The Burning Bush told me that I must unite the animals against evil," answered Lion Ascend with trepidation in his voice.

There was a moment of silence that Lion Ascend didn't expect to have as he lie down in front of the cheetah. He spent the time looking at Nikkita as she lay across from him and felt her eyes melt into his. He wished that things were different for him, but they weren't.

"I made a new friend, her name is Dafidale and she wants to help you," replied Nikkita.

"That's nice, but I don't see how she can help me."

"She has amazing powers," interrupted Nikkita as she heard howls. Nikkita looked around in the direction of the howls and wondered if they were getting a visit.

"Have you kept yourself safe from danger Lion Ascend?" asked a familiar voice.

Lion Ascend rose to his feet just as Nikkita did and turned his head to see that it was the white wolf and smiled. Abel looked at the lion gallantly with his blue eyes and slowly walked over to him. Each step was slow as well as placid as he crept close to Lion Ascend.

"I have kept myself safe Abel," answered Lion Ascend.

"What news do you bring us general?" asked Lobby as he stopped wrestling with his brother.

"Tomorrow is a big day for the lion. It will be a big day for all of us," declared Abel.

"I wish there was more that I could do," declared Lion Ascend as he looked down.

"You will know what you must do after tomorrow," answered Abel.

"Why is that? LA was visited by the Burning Bush. He knows exactly what to do," said Nikkita confidently.

General Abel looked at Nikkita and then continued, "the wild dogs will be coming for you and the wolves will be holding them back. The training by Iza will help you, but the visit from the Burning Bush is something to remarkable for any of us to interpret."

Lion Ascend watched the white wolf run back the way he came in through the distance and disappear in the woods. Abel was risking his life to protect him and a sense of numbness came over Lion Ascend. He felt it in the ground, smelled it in the rocks and saw it in the cheetah's eyes. Something powerful had just taken place; the animals of Everlow were going to fight tomorrow so he could live and get his training.

The sun disappeared in the horizon and the moon emerged in the sky like many times before. Nikkita saw something was bothering Lion Ascend. She tried to think of what could be done to ease his mind from the weight of the world. After looking up at the moon she turned around to walk back to the den to lie down and sleep.

*The cheetah walked around through the meadow and looked up at the*
*starlit sky as well as the moon. Suddenly, she turned around from a very bright fire and saw Dafidale standing in front of her. She was dressed in silver leaves which illuminated with brightness.*

*"How did you find me?" asked Nikkita.*

*"Love isn't hard to find when your star projecting," replied Dafidale.    "Star projecting, what's that?"*

*"I'll explain that another time. Do you have something you want to share with Lion Ascend?" asked the Xera.*

*"Yes, but I don't think I can," answered Nikkita.*

*"I'll help you," Dafidale said softly.*

*Nikkita turned around to see Lion Ascend stepping out of the entrance of the cave and walked up to the Xera. He looked curiously at the creature and wondered who she was. Nikkita looked at Lion Ascend and knew what had to be done. The words came to play as she remembered what to say.*

*"Lion Ascend before you speak I want you to know*

something," replied Nikkita as she looked into his eyes and prepared to sing;

The wind brushes against my veil as I see you in the distance
You look so happy, you look so pale as though you are disappearing from existence.
I enter your world with the coldness that bites my skin
You've been abused; you've been alone with nowhere to turn
It's like the craters on the moon and the desert that lies here to sin
You can tell me what you wish, let everything consume with fire and burn
And I will still remain the cheetah

I'm the sun you're the moon
let the wind brush us away soon
I'll walk on the moon and plant my rose
we'll watch it grow and change us forever
go for your dreams, go for your destiny, go for the love that's high above
for you're the lion and I'm the cheetah

remember the laughter, remember the dreams where everything is what it seems
I'll take your pain if you'll accept my tears
unfold its wings and I'll blow you a kiss
in a world full of vultures and nothing is what it seems
my heart is glass, hidden in my chest with all the cares of our world
put together the pieces for the enigma of your fears
others upon Ayana are waiting to smash our dreams
love me like the moon loves the sun for I shall always be apart of your world
and I will still remain the cheetah

*you're the sun, I'm the moon*
*let the wind brush us away soon*
*I'll walk on the moon and plant my rose*
*we'll watch it grow and change us forever*
*go for your dreams, go for your destiny, go for the love*
*that's high above*
*for you're the lion and I'm the cheetah*


*"That was beautiful," replied Lion Ascend, as he returned his attention to the Xera. "Who is this?"*

*"This is my friend Dafidale," replied Nikkita.*

*"There is much to discuss my young prince. You're important in this war," declared Dafidale.*

*"Where do you fit in all of this? Whose side are you on?" asked Lion Ascend.*

*"I'm a healer and messenger, I'm on your side. It's been hundreds of years since I've seen a lion. A few of them have been captured in the Black Catacomb."*

*"How will I find you?" asked Lion Ascend.*

*Dafidale cracked a grin, "I'll find you, my lord. All you have to do is pray."*

*Lion Ascend watched the Xera open her large wings and quickly fly up through the air. She hovered brightly over the forest and disappeared over the trees in the distance. The lion turned his head to Nikkita who nodded her head. He looked up at the moon that filled the night sky and watched everything fade away.*

The great lion opened his eyes and realized he had been dreaming once again. He looked up to the moon; then to Nikkita who was sound asleep. He smiled with the memory of what she sang in the dream. Soon it would be morning and a new day would begin. The lion laid down to wait for the sun; he began thinking about the Xera that had visited. He fell asleep not realizing that today was the beginning of his new life.

The sun peered over the trees and the cats continued to sleep. Lion Ascend slowly opened his eyes to the day of training. It was morning; the cubs were over a year old and the same size as their mother except Lion Ascend who was the size as a horse. Something was obviously different about him from the moment he was a cub to the grown lion at present. His mother could see that true courage was yet to be found, but he held the integrity of having a good heart.  Vera began thinking of worrisome questions; would he be brave enough to stop the tigers and bring freedom to the land? Mother cheetah ceased with the negative thinking and began with the thoughts of knowing this day would come and that Lion Ascend would inspire the animals of the world.

Abel and Enoch were present with Iza and looked proudly at Vera for taking care of the lion. Iza looked at Lion Ascend and saw how much he had grown. The Priest of Pride marveled at the lion's size. He couldn't believe how well the prophecy foretold the lion's description.

"I'm very proud that Lion Ascend has made it this far with you," replied Iza.

"It's been an honor to protect him," answered Vera as she looked at her children.

"The day is young and the age is right, it's time to put up a fight," replied the Priest of Pride.

"Will he be strong enough to travel with you through the darkest territory of the forest, to the mountains where he will be trained?" asked Vera.

"Yes," answered Iza.

"Lion Ascend must be trained immediately to protect Everlow," continued Iza as he nodded his head at Vera.

"But is it wise to travel while it's light?" Vera's voice trembled as her eyes looked worried.

"The path we shall walk on is free from evil," assured Iza.

The anxiety filled Vera in the form of tightness in her

shoulders and the trembling was unveiled with the sound of whining from her stomach. Lion Ascend walked over to her and nuzzled his head into hers. "I'll be fine, I'm doing what is needed and I'll be back before you know it." Vera nodded as she looked into his eyes and her eyes welled up with tears. Lion Ascend was her son and the thought of uncertainty emerged; he could be lost forever. The great lion stepped up to Iza to hear what needed to be done.

"Once we get to the cave, The Winds of Change, he will be trained well and take his place as lord of the animals," said Iza.

"How long is the training?" asked Lion Ascend.

"The training is as long as you wish it," answered Iza.

"I'm coming with you," declared Nikkita as she sat down next to the two cats. Her face was stern as she stared into Lion Ascend's eyes expecting to be refused. The Priest of Pride knew that there was not going to be a way to talk her out of it; he sensed the love she had for the lion.

"Nikkita! You're my only daughter, I forbid you to go, you could get hurt or die!" exclaimed her mother.

"Mother, I know the risks, I want to be there to witness this greatness in history. I'm old enough to make my own decisions and I'm going with Lion Ascend," she answered while turning her head from Vera's trembling lips back to Lion Ascend.

All was silent until the Priest of Pride spoke. He felt in his heart that if Nikkita went along, Lion Ascend would learn his special abilities faster. In this child's eyes, he felt, she would inspire the lion to be courageous and deliver his unyielding power against the tigers. Vera's mouth slowly dropped for she didn't want to lose her only daughter to the outside world. The mother lowered her head to the ground realizing that her brood had grown and weren't weak to the world around her. Nikkita would be fine and capable of defending herself.

"She can come, but she can't interfere with the changes that will come upon Lion Ascend," commanded Iza

"I agree and I accept," smiled Nikkita with a nod while looking at LA. "Somebody has to keep you company," she continued with a smile.

"Hey, what about us?" demanded Lobby.

"Lobby, Chalice I need you here to protect the den from any uninvited guests," replied Lion Ascend.

"You could assist me against the dark forces of Cain," began General Abel as he turned to Iza and Enoch with a nod. "We've got a plan," continued the white wolf. "To hold back the wild dogs at bay with the high numbers of wolves, albatrosses and eagles. We could use your son's help to fight the tigers and seek out those that can carry on our rebellion."

Lobby and Chalice looked at each other with satisfaction. They were excited to join the resistance, but were unsure of how to act in their inspiration. It was a feeling of doing something great that was glorious, but with no words to describe it. "I can't speak for my sons, for they must make there own decisions," answered Vera slowly realizing from her conversation with Nikkita that they were old enough to make their own decisions. Lion Ascend grinned and felt joy that he was getting all this help.

"Abel what can we do to help?" asked Chalice.

"Come back with me to plan our defense against the wild dogs," encouraged General Abel as he a smiled.

"We must go now," said the Priest of Pride.

"I'm ready," said the lion as he followed Iza down the deep slope accompanied with Nikkita.

They left the den to go somewhere far away and for the first time in a long time Lion Ascend felt scared. It seemed that they were walking for miles, through the forests and meadow. They walked through scorched pine trees and heard the sounds of crickets. They passed the sight of corpse and saw the shapes of deceased animals along the ground. The lion smelled the bones and looked around at the trees that loomed in despair.

"Something bad happened here years ago," began Lion Ascend.

"What?" whispered Nikkita.

"There are skeletal remains of wolves, lions, hyenas and tigers. There was a war here," whispered Lion Ascend emotionally as his ears perked up to a distant howling from behind and wondered what was going on. It became their territory to travel in the foreign land of evil with the bright sun shining on their back.

"Where is this Winds of Change?" whispered Nikkita.

"We'll be there tomorrow," answered Iza as he turned around.

"You know that isn't fair, I was asking Lion Ascend, not you," griped Nikkita

"The more you stop and talk the quicker we'll be caught by the tigers," replied Iza.

"We could be caught now, I smell coyotes, hyenas and jackals in these dead woods," answered Nikkita.

"You smell dead animals that gave there lives for this day to come," declared the Priest of Pride.

The wild dogs knew about the trio's journey and were already tracking them down to stop the prophecy from becoming reality. The Priest of Pride realized it every step of the way until they suddenly came to a river. Iza remained at a halt for a moment then continued with his slow walk to hide their tracks in the water. Lion Ascend watched the white cougar swim through the violent rips of current. Nikkita could hear the wolves howl in the distance behind them. There were dozens of cries from the wolves that were off to war. Once Iza was across the river he shook his white cloak and looked at the lion and cheetah. The lion made it and shook his golden mane from the water and turned around as he wondered what new challenges awaited him. Iza stood before the two cats, looking directly into Lion Ascend's eyes. "You will have your challenge, "assured Iza as he looked at Nikkita who was confused. Lion Ascends' eyes widened with startled amazement for he had been thinking about the challenges. Nikkita looked at Lion Ascend with amazement as her eyebrows lifted, but she said nothing. It was pretty obvious that Iza had the power of a prophet.

The trio made there way through a thin layer of forest and soon golden plains were in the distance. A queer mountain stood before them. Together they could see reflecting glitters of light from the sun. They were left astonished and surprised after their exhausting travel through the night. "The Winds of Change" said the Priest of Pride. Lion Ascend and Nikkita looked at the mountain and smiled because it was an answer to their prayers.

The sun shone over the fifty wolves that grouped at Vera's old den to assemble for the battle. Forty eagles landed upon the trees as well as twenty albatrosses to listen to General Abel's plan of attack.

"Sampson is going to lead only twenty of our numbers. I want Avian's group to attack from the north. Knightly's group from the West, Kayda's from the East. My group will attack from the South. Enoch, I want you to assemble your numbers to hide in the tree tops. Once the wild dogs are inside the perimeter of Vera's old den, we'll attack and they'll be cut off. Only I give the sound of retreat! Any questions?" asked Abel.

"How many wild dogs are coming?" asked Sampson.

Abel was a little worried, "I don't know, probably more than seventy. These beasts have no sympathy or remorse. I'm not going to stand here and draw a pretty picture on the ground that everything will be alright. Today we fight and tomorrow we'll fight again against the tigers!"

There were cheers and howls from the wolves that could be heard for miles. Lobby and Chalice had just returned from scouting the perimeter and faced the white wolf that looked at them anxiously, waiting to hear what they had discovered.

"They're massing in the distance," protested Lobby.

"The time is now," replied Abel as he nodded for Sampson to lure the wild dogs inside the perimeter. The eagles took position in the top of the trees as the albatrosses hid deeper in the woods to conceal there presence. Abel looked around to make sure his troops were all accounted for until he was approached by the cheetahs.

"Where should we go?" asked Chalice.

"Come with me," he replied as he led the cheetahs with the group of wolves.

Sampson walked from the edge of the forest to see a small

army in the distance. The wild dogs began marching, there were seventy-five slowly closing in on Sampson's small contingent. The red wolf let out a howl for his father and the other wolves began to howl with him not knowing if it would be their last. The wild dogs began to growl in the distance and the coyotes also howled to proclaim their victory over the wolves.

"Steady my brothers and sisters," commanded Sampson as he watched the dark army draw close. Cain was in front and had a big sneer on his face as he saw how small an army Sampson had. This would be a quick victory.

"Looks to me, you better start running young pup. Twenty wolves is no match for an army over seventy-five," he laughed.

Sampson ignored him and concentrated on how far the wild dogs were. Talick looked at the other wolves suspiciously as he waited for the order from their leader. What were they waiting for? Talick thought.

"Now!" exclaimed Sampson as all the wolves retreated deep into the woods. The hyenas growled and charged after the wolves. Cain led his army through the first group of trees protected by the wolves. Nothing was going to come between the wild dogs and the killing of Lion Ascend. "Kill the cowards!" commanded Cain. "Kill all that's in your path!  Find the lion and kill him!"

Seventy-five of the wild dogs began barking and growling as they ripped through the brush. They were led by the twenty wolves to Vera's old den in the clearing, deep in the forest of Everlow. Cain watched the wolves wait patiently in a group as the wild dogs surrounded them. It seemed suspicious and too easy to kill the small contingent.     Suddenly they were ambushed by wolves from all different directions. Eagles swooped low with their sharp talons and shed blood upon many of the hyenas. Albatrosses swooped in to pick up four or five of the wild dogs and tossed them through the air as though they were small trees.

Abel charged through the battle to witness each fight between wolf and beast to get an overview of the attack. The general found himself hindered when Talick jumped on him. With the thrust of Abel's fierce sabers, he ripped the flesh from the creature's muzzle and punctured his right arm. After hearing Talick yelp in pain, a group of five coyotes charged after General Abel. Avian jumped in front of his father and the coyotes attacked him instead.

The wolves felt confident when they realized they were holding the wild dogs off. Abel looked into Enoch's eyes and wondered if today they would remain standing. The sun remained over head and they wondered how long the battle would last. The wild dogs were no match for the albatrosses and the eagles were formidable adversaries. Cain stepped through the ending of the forest towards the mountains where Lion Ascend had left and was met by Chalice.

"You shall not pass," growled Chalice.

"You're just a cub. You're much too young for me to bother."

"Am I? Was it not too long ago that you ordered the death of my brother, Lion Ascend?"

Seconds passed as Cain licked his lips. "So be it!" bellowed Cain as he charged after the cheetah. Chalice swiped his claws into the hyena's face and bit Cain's shoulder. All at once Lobby, who was hiding behind a tree, jumped on top of the hyena's back and dug his teeth as well as his claws into the enemy's hide. Cain yelped in pain while moving in all directions and swiped his right paw in Chalice's face. The beast gripped hold of Lobby's head with his arms and bucked Lobby off his back. Both cheetahs were exhausted as they lay next to a tree.

"Who would have thought a hyena could defeat two cheetahs; Two cheetahs defending a lion that left his land. I think this calls for a special honor that should be resolved in your death, don't you agree?" laughed Cain as he was about to charge.

"Cheetah's are never afraid! We stick together, always!" exclaimed Lobby.

"I doubt it, where is your mother so I may kill her too," sneered Cain.

Lobby and Chalice were surprised to see a shadow leap

from the branches. It was Vera with skills of fighting beyond the cub's years. She snarled in rage upon the culprit that vowed to kill her. She fought Cain with such agility and quickness of her sharp claws ripping the wounds wider that were already open. Lobby and Chalice joined Vera in the fight to kill Cain.

The battle continued as the wolves increased their numbers upon the wild dogs that continued to fight. The creatures of the tiger's empire began to retreat out of the forest to escape a battle they would never win. Abel could hear the surrender from many of the wild dogs that were still alive. The general looked around after ripping a hyena's throat, to see many of the wolves chasing the wild dogs out of Everlow. The white wolf looked up to the sky with blood soaked in his fur around his mouth while letting out a howl and lowered it as a drop of blood slowly fell from his mouth.

"Father, we should continue the pursuit!" exclaimed Knightly.

"No, let them go!" commanded Abel as he watched his son, the speckled grey and white wolf, leave and let out a howl.

"We're winning," said Kayda with a smile.

Abel looked at Kayda, his daughter with the white fur with the black on the end. He smiled as he realized that their enemies were gone, but knew there would be many battles to fight.

"Call off the pursuit and let's tend to our wounded," ordered Abel.

"Yes father," answered Kayda as she let out a howl to call off her team.

Cain wrestled with the three cheetahs when he heard the wolves howling and knew the battle was lost. His efforts to kill Abel and hunt down Lion Ascend were over Cain backed away from Vera as he heard her snarl and growl at him.

"Perhaps another time," began Cain as he watched the last of his army flee from view with the pursuit of the wolves. His fangs sneered over his lower lip and his brown eyes leered at the cowards that called themselves warriors.

"I will have my revenge!" he exclaimed as he fled in the

distance behind the trees.

Lobby and Chalice were about to go after him when Vera stood in the way. "Let him go. We won and should be thankful that we're alive."

Suddenly, the clouds began to veil the sun and sprinkles of rain fell upon their faces. Vera let the sprinkles fall upon her wounds as tears of joy were embraced with the thought of victory. The wild dogs had been defeated, but at what cost?

A tear fell from Abel; Avian lay dead and mutilated upon the grass soaked with blood. The white wolf let out a howl while the feeling of lightning coursed up and down his spine. His children met with him and howled in memory of their brother Avian.

The sun shined brightly upon the trio as they walked around the mountainous region. The granite rocks sparkled brightly into Lion Ascend's eyes from the reflection of the sun. Nikkita looked around with enthusiasm and wondered what adventure awaited them.

The lion and the cheetah kept walking behind Iza as they saw the amount of trees in the area lessen. Their roots were twisted into the rock and it reminded Lion Ascend of how special it was to have a strong foundation. The great cat turned around to see how high they were and could see the small forest in the distance. Everlow Forest seemed so small and insignificant to the measure of what he would be fighting for. He could feel the aching in his feet and was too tired to move. His stomach whined and felt the need to retire from such a long walk.

"We need to stop," yelled Lion Ascend.

"Why?" asked Iza as he turned around from a distance.

"It's going to get dark soon. We can continue this at the break of dawn," answered Lion Ascend.

Iza was quiet and agreed that it would be best not to exhaust Lion Ascend. "We'll take a break for now," replied Iza.

"It's so beautiful," smiled Nikkita as she looked at Everlow Forest.

"Yes it is, I would give anything to be home again than to

climb this mountain in front of us," answered Lion Ascend as he continued to look at the challenge before him.

"Oh, LA, it can't be that bad," she began while turning her head to see the mountain that was before them. "Oh wow! That's a big mountain," said Nikkita. She was dreading the climb and they both looked at each other, then to the Priest of Pride. His eyes were still, a pale blue had engulfed his eyes; it seemed he was a world apart. "In this journey, there are four challenges that await you, strength, speed, wisdom, and courage. This challenge is the test of strength. You may proceed," replied Iza

"Tomorrow, early in the morning, my kind sir," answered Lion Ascend.

"You say tomorrow morning? I order you to climb it now! Only cowards procrastinate," declared Iza.

"Are you calling me a coward!" growled Lion Ascend as his eyebrows protruded.

Iza remained quiet and unchallenging. He knew something in the land, the streams, the forest that Lion Ascend didn't and that the Burning Bush predicted the
prophecy of a courageous lion uniting the animals of the land.

"You can't possibly be serious about climbing this mountain. It's too rugged and steep to climb," continued Lion Ascend.

"It's the test of your abilities and to train you against the impossible," answered the Priest of Pride as he waited for Lion Ascend to begin.

Lion Ascend looked at his best friend for support, but all he got was a shrug. She didn't know what to do, since this adventure was unlike anything she had experienced. "Well, I suppose we better get started," replied Nikkita as she looked into his eyes and inspired him.

Lion Ascend turned around to the mountain and walked over to it. It was a rugged mountain that shot straight up to the sky and there was little to grip. Nikkita stood next to him and looked up the rocky edge of torrent rock. "I have faith in you, Climb this challenge and show him that you can do it!" she exclaimed.

# Lion Ascend

"Turn back! Turn back Lion Ascend! If you truly believe you can not overpower this obstacle and become king of the animals!" began Iza in a yell. "Then you're not who  I thought you were in legend!"

The lion looked at the cougar and thought how much of a fool he was. It seemed strange that the one cat that would believe in him would insult him. LA turned his head to Nikkita who nodded with a light smile. This cheetah believed in him and knew the cost of climbing a mountain after many days of walking. She would not be able to climb the mountain with him, but she would inspire him. "I'll find a way to the crest and I promise you will reach the top," she said with fire of determination in her voice.

Lion Ascend turned his head to the base of the mountain. His paws were big, his claws were sharp, his limbs were strong and his eyes were keen enough to look ahead to make each leap. "I accept your challenge!" replied Lion Ascend. With a big thrust from his hind legs he gripped the first indention of the rock. Minutes passed with each climb, he looked above the trees and saw the beautiful green prairies. The wind brushed up against his golden mane as he felt the cool wind run against his nose. He took a deep breath as the rich smell of ice and the forest became a part of him. Lion Ascend looked down to see that Nikkita and Iza were gone. The lion felt his sharp claws shift along the rock and lifted his robust body to each ledge of the mountain. It was still day light, but he began to realize as he progressed so did the cold winds. The complete exhilaration of being so high made him feel that he could fly. Pictures emerged in his mind of the good times he had with Nikkita.

*It was a time of innocence for the cubs, a time to play and forget about their worries. Lion Ascend was chasing after Nikkita in a game called cat and mouse. Nikkita was to busy laughing at Lion Ascend to get away.*

*"I'm going to get you!" roared the young cub as he was inches from her long tail.*

*"You'll never catch me LA because you're a lion*

*and I'm a cheetah." "Well, I've been doing a very good job keeping up to you. At least I'm not*

*afraid to catch you," laughed Lion Ascend.*

*Suddenly, Nikkita increased her speed and was able to get behind a tree. Every time Lion Ascend walked around the tree to catch up to her she would keep running. The echo of laughter was so powerful that it intoxicated the lion. He was getting dizzy running in circles around the trunk of the tree.*

*"Getting tired LA?" laughed the cheetah as she jumped over the collapsed lion.*

*"Why do you have to be difficult?" he asked.*

*"Difficult?" she said.*

*"Teasing me because I can't catch you," said Lion Ascend.*

*"Oh, don't be a fool! We all have our place in the world. My place is to be the good hearted cheetah, to be the comforter as well as the hunter. Don't you remember? Have a good heart."*

*"There doesn't seem to be a place for a lion," answered Lion Ascend sadly. Nikkita looked into his sad eyes and knew that something was wrong. "You'll always have a place in my heart. Now, I'm willing to bet that if you tried hard enough you could catch me!" she said as she cracked a grin.*

*Lion Ascend sprung up to catch the running cheetah. He felt the muscles in his back and legs tighten up, but in slow motion he felt his paws touch her torso. He playfully gripped her shoulder with his jaw and they both tumbled to the ground. "You let me catch you," laughed the lion as he stared into her eyes. The light chuckles of laughter consumed his ears as he watched her eyes close. "I'm tired, surely you can understand a creature built for speed can only run so far before she gets exhausted,"*

*replied Nikkita.*
*"Right, I'm sure every cheetah says that,"*
*answered Lion Ascend.*
*"It's true, I'm tired of running!"*
*"Good, tag you're it!" laughed the lion as he ran*
*away and heard the groaning laughter of Nikkita as she got*
*up to pursue him.*

It was a beautiful flash back and it made Lion Ascend
realize his purpose. He was a lion and he was built for an entirely
different function. Climbing the mountain suddenly became much
easier. He was almost to the top and looked above to see the
horizon in the distance, the forest, a mountain range and a smell of
the ocean.

He looked around to see a small pool of crystal water
nearby. There was a cave carved into the rock just ahead and
beyond that a range of mountains in the background. Two cats
emerged from the distance of the mountain and as they grew
larger, he realized it was Iza and Nikkita. There eyes widened as
they watched the golden aura emerge from Lion Ascend's crown.

"You have completed the test of strength," replied Iza.

"Then I've proven myself?" asked the tired lion.

"Yes," answered Iza.

Nikkita's eyes widened to Lion Ascend's aura and his
incredible achievement.
The lion looked into Nikkita's eyes as he rested to catch his breath
and felt very tired. He walked past the Priest of Pride to find a spot
to lie down and fell asleep right away.

The battle was won as the sun set upon the mountains in the
west. A total of eleven wolves had been killed and six were
severely wounded. Enoch reported that fifteen eagles had been
wounded and four were killed. Abel turned his head to see the
family of cheetahs walking out of their old den. They were
wounded from the chest, but they were walking proudly. Abel's
blue eyes looked down to the ground in sadness for Avian was
gone. He fought well protecting his father from a group of coyotes

that would have ripped him apart.

"Is it over?" asked a familiar voice.

Abel looked up at mother cheetah and breathed in deeply through his nose. "The battle is over, but the war is far from ending. We're not ready to take on another attack," answered the white wolf.

"Then we'll win, won't we! I'm not going to surrender to the Tyrone!" exclaimed Vera.

"I've fought many wars including one with your husband, Rythemic. I will not pursue the wild dogs with less than fifty wolves. Not even for you!" growled Abel as he got up to meet with Enoch alone.

The white wolf walked as far as the edge of Everlow Forest with a sour taste in his mouth. He should have expected that there would have been casualties, but he didn't expect to bury one of his sons. In the distance he watched the moon emerge while the sun disappeared behind him in the trees. Suddenly, the flapping of wings was heard next to him and it was Enoch. "Sir, we've completed our last round of sweeps. The wild dogs have retreated to the Bad Lands."

"Excellent work Enoch! Lets hope they won't come back," said Abel.

"I hope so my lord."

"I hope this battle has given Lion Ascend the chance for his training," said Abel as he watched smoke fill the sky from the volcanoes. The enemy would be back and they would be accompanied by the tigers. Abel hoped that Lion Ascend would return in time to face the wickedness of the tigers.

Deep in the depths of the Bad Lands, Cain and his followers retreated to the stronghold of Tyrone. The dead volcano held hundreds of tigers, wild dogs and other dark flying creatures. They all watched the remainder of the wild dogs enter through the large crowds and walk towards the throne. Tyrone looked very displeased at the sight of Cain and his followers. "You look like you traveled through a garden of wicker plants," said Tyrone.

"My lord we were ambushed by the wolves, cheetahs,

eagles and albatrosses. We were no match for them," Cain pleaded as a defense.

"No match," began Tyrone as he rose up and stretched his back legs to begin walking towards the hyena. With a quick thrust of his paw he struck the hyena in the face and let out a snarl. "You have over seventy wild dogs and you're telling me you were defeated?" shouted the tiger.

"Yes my lord," answered Cain quietly.

"Sir, it's true we were ambushed by more numbers than we were prepared to fight," replied Talick as he limped forward.

"Shut up! You idiot," growled Tyrone as he returned to his comfortable spot of sitting. "My superiors are out conquering other parts of Ayana and I'm struggling to take over this patch of forest. King Estargo has over a thousand tigers helping him and Prince Voltar has five-hundred and here I have three hundred tigers, five hundred wild dogs and about six-hundred hawks and crows combined. You're telling me that a small number of wolves defeated you?" bellowed Tyrone as his yellow snake like eyes stared dead into Cain's.

"Yes my lord," answered the hyena with a voice trembling in fear.

"Well then, I guess what I have to do is figure out who I need to eliminate, to press the message that Everlow belongs to me," said Tyrone, knowing he was sending a message of fear to all his followers. "Sir?" asked Cain as he looked into the tiger's wicked sneer and watched the wheels turn behind his eyes.

It was now night and a dozen wolves had returned with food. The cheetahs shared in the hospitality. Abel was sitting near Avian's grave telling him that everything would be ok and that he didn't die in vain. All of a sudden there was a strange light towards the west, which was too bright to be the sunset.

"What's that?" asked Sampson as he looked at his siblings then to his father.

The light eventually dimmed and a beautiful creature remained. She had long sandy brown hair and her face was shaped like a monkey. Her arms were long with no fur or hair and silver leaves covered her chest and torso. Her naked legs reflected the pale moon with every step as she proceeded towards the white wolf.

The white wolf walked over to smell the rich aroma of lilacs and roses that covered the creature. She looked enchantingly, with her warm eyes, at the wolf and slowly reached her hand out to touch his head. Abel stepped back and avoided her hand with distrust.

"Forgive me if I've startled you my lord, but I've only come to heal you and the injured," she replied as her hand returned.

"Who are you?" asked Abel.

"Oh, forgive me, where are my manners? My name is Dafidale, Queen of the Xeras."

"What's a Xera?" asked Abel.

"We're fairies, the keepers of balance. We do as we have done for thousands of years to serve the Burning Bush's wishes of balance for the continent of Copper Toe as well as the world of Ayana. Right now is a fragile moment in history where Lion Ascend has to decide the fate of us all," answered Dafidale as she knelt down eye level to Abel.

"You know about the prophecy?" asked Abel.

"I knew about the prophecy hundreds of years ago and have waited for this moment to help those who serve the creator," said Dafidale

Abel began walking closer to her and felt the white illumination from her hand

shower upon his face like the gaze of the sun. He felt a powerful thrust of tingling to his belly that loosened the knot of anger for the loss of his son. Dafidale touched Abel's head slowly and circled her finger around his ears. Numerous amounts of light emerged from her through the night and flew around the animals as the sound of harps played with the voice that sounded angelic. The sound of voices sung in interlude to the fragile distraught wolves and eagles that were feeling emotionally drained from the battle.

Dafidale stretched both her arms into the air as her huge white wings spread apart for the animals to see.

The sky began to rumble while the wind began to run through shrubs and brush. Dafidale's sandy brown hair flew up against her beautiful face and collar bone as she closed her brown eyes. She lowered her right arm and pointed to a circle of rocks.

"Let there be fire," she commanded as her voice echoed through the night. Then lightning struck to where she pointed, unleashing a fire. This got the cheetahs attention and it quickly grew for all the animals to keep warm. Dafidale re-opened her eyes and opened her mouth to sing a song that would heal such troubled hearts.

*I know I could hold you*
*in the way that I would love too*
*my journey is so incomplete*
*your life is so complete*
*it makes me sad to say goodbye*
*I set you free to fly*
*to fly away*
*I loved you too dearly but I will adore you*
*forever as yours I will understand, I will understand!*
*the reason to hold you like a memory*
*do you remember the days we laughed?*
*do you remember the days we cried?*
*do you remember the day you stayed?*
*do you remember the day you were at my side?*
*I loved you too much*
*to hold you like a memory*
*to keep you as a memory*

Abel and Enoch looked at each other then to the Xera as her song came to a close. She was unlike anything they had ever seen and it was clear that the Xeras were good creatures. They felt free from the despair of the death of their loved ones and would be able to carry on the fight. Abel walked over to Dafidale and looked into her eyes, "thank you."

"The pain in your hearts has been released. When you wake up tomorrow I'll be gone, but I won't be forgotten," she answered with a grin. The group of animals rejoiced with the Xeras as the clouds veiled the full moon. Tomorrow would be a brand new day

and for the first time Abel felt closure for his son, Avian.

The cool winds of dawn arrived and Lion Ascend's eyes opened to see the sun gaze from the east. A smile emerged upon the lion's face as a string of mane touched his brow. He raised himself up to stretch his hind legs and turned to see his companions were gone. Lion Ascend turned his head and saw the cheetah dragging a dead deer gripped in her mouth. She snugged the beast's neck with her sharp teeth and dropped it just before the lion.

"My offering Lion Ascend, you're hungry and need strength for the next challenge."

Lion Ascend looked at her, "I appreciate your offer, but since my meeting with the Burning Bush I can no longer eat the flesh of an innocent animal. If I had a choice I would rather eat a tiger or hyena," he began.

"Of course you can eat; it's what we do to survive! There's no honor in feeling guilty for killing when you're a hunter," said Nikkita.

"I'm sorry, but I can't. Maybe another time in the future when the time permits it," replied Lion Ascend.

"Well then what will you eat?" she asked.

Lion Ascend smiled and ran away leaving her confused, "I'll show you what I like to eat," he said.

The day continued and she waited for Lion Ascend to return while eating her food. Nikkita continued to eat the dead carcass just as a couple of round fruits dropped before her. She looked at Lion Ascend, "you must be joking."

"Wow, these are good," she said while eating them. Nikkita looked up to see him smiling at her. Lion Ascend bit into another one with his teeth and sucked the juices before eating it.

He left to get more and was finished eating just as she was with her deer.

The lion lay in the sun and was day dreaming of the past. The memories cascaded through his mind like lightning thrusting the ground and he quickly got up. The memory of Vera rescuing him from Jezebel surfaced.

"What's the matter?" asked Nikkita.

"Nothing, I was just thinking of how lucky I was to be in your family." Nikkita hadn't forgotten those old times of laughter and being told to have a good heart by Vera.         "The honor was ours," she replied.

"Nikkita, I only wish to protect everyone. I fear the tigers will destroy Everlow," he answered.

"You're wrong! Everyday you walk the land brings the tigers closer to defeat."

The conversation came to a halt when Iza stepped near them. Lion Ascend turned his head to the cougar just as Nikkita did. "The Beast of Speed awaits you," said Iza. Lion Ascend was silent as he took a deep breath and looked up to the sky. The miraculous curly clouds unfolded upon themselves in the form of cats while the wind blew in his face. He could feel the swarm of butterflies fill his insides as well as the trembling in his legs.

The words echoed in his head like a pebble falling inside of a cave and into a pond. How fast is fast? What did the beast look like? Was there a chance of success? The questions jumbled in his mind.

"What must I do?" asked Lion Ascend.

"You must go into the cave to retrieve a jewel that is hidden in the grips of the dragon," answered the Priest of Pride.

"Is there a chance I'll succeed?" asked Lion Ascend, but didn't get the answer he wanted.

"If you fail, Everlow Forest will fall to the tigers and Ayana will descend in darkness."

Lion Ascend turned his head to Nikkita and could see she didn't want to lose him. He turned his head and began walking slowly to the entrance of the cave to face the dragon.

"LA, don't throw your life away!" cried Nikkita.

"Silence!" growled Iza as he stood in front of her.

"You gave me your word that you wouldn't interfere in his training!"

Nikkita was silent and after looking into Lion Ascend's eyes, she realized he had to do this. Each step of the way Nikkita watched him step inside the cave and felt her heart beat faster.

He walked around the inside of the cave and saw numerous claw marks on the rocks. Skeletons on the floor and Lion Ascend lowered his head to smell them. An elevated ripping sound was heard in the distance of the cave and he perked his ears up. It was dark, but Lion Ascend could see in the dark better than during the day. The beast was here inside the grotto waiting for him as a hunter waits for its prey. The lion continued the walk through the cave and somehow knew that anyone who tried to slay the Beast of Speed ultimately failed. The bones he sniffed earlier belonged to the cheetahs and wolves. Lion Ascend stumbled upon an open chamber where he saw a golden colored crystal, which made a ringing sound. As he crept closer to the jewel, he heard something scratch the walls and breathe. LA could feel the cold sensation rivet through his legs and shoulders. The feeling of evil surrounded him waiting to strike without hesitation. His eyes turned to the right then to the left to see a set of red eyes stare back at him. As quick as possible, Lion Ascend struck the beast with his retractable claws. He gripped the jewel with his mouth; dodged the snapping jaws of the beast and ran out the way he came in.

The cheetah and the cougar heard growls, tip taps and breathing. A shriek passed through their ears as well as a roar that echoed throughout the cave. The quick charge echoed from the walls of the cave. Soon Lion Ascend began to emerge from out of the darkness. The giant head of a serpent with claws came out from behind the lion trying to eat him whole.

The Beast of Speed was completely out of the cave and was still pursuing the lion with its giant wings spanned out. Lion Ascend dropped the gem just before the Priest of Pride and looked up at the wounded creature. It looked like a giant lizard with green scales and a design of stars upon its skin. The long sharp claws from the dragon got Lion

Ascend's attention as well as the large white teeth and the wound could be seen on the creature's forehead.

"I command you to desist and return back into the cave!" commanded Iza.

"I obey no one!" snarled the Beast of Speed.

"You shall do so under the command of the Burning Bush," roared Iza as he looked up at the beast.

"I demand the possession of my jewel! Give it to me, now!" exclaimed the beast as it jumped up and down on its four legs.

"Give him the jewel," ordered the Priest of Pride.

Lion Ascend looked at Iza as though he was crazy, but proceeded. He picked up the jewel; walked over to the serpent and hoped that he wouldn't become dinner. He dropped the jewel before the dragon as it growled at him. "You're a lion?" asked the Beast of Speed.

"Yes I am," Lion Ascend answered.

"I was told by the Priest of Pride that a lion would be brave enough to enter and escape the cave with my jewel without being eaten and that this lion would also be brave enough to fight the tigers."

Lion Ascend looked at the ground as he tried to understand what the dragon was saying. Something in the dragon's voice was irritating and annoying. The dragon was hidden deep in a cave. He was capable of killing the tigers, but preferred to do nothing.

"Are you not a lion?" repeated the beast.

"I am," answered Lion Ascend.

"Then let me hear you roar!"

Lion Ascend turned around to his friends and saw Nikkita smiling at him. His yellow eyes turned to the Beast of Speed who was waiting to hear the roar in the clear open air. Lion Ascend let out a roar from deep within his chest. It was loud as well as vibrant and echoed through the mountains.

The dragon nodded while picking up the jewel and placed it near him, "I haven't seen a lion for a thousand years."

"Well, now you have. What's your name?" asked Lion Ascend.

"What's yours?" asked the beast.

"My friends call me LA."

"My name is Bizare and I'm pleased to meet you, but if you don't mind, I must be going," replied Bizarre as he began walking back to the cave.

Lion Ascend turned to look at Iza and Nikkita and knew that he had won the challenge. The sun was overhead and Lion Ascend didn't want it to end. Something in his heart was telling him to make amends with the dragon.

"Hey!" yelled Lion Ascend to Bizare, who turned his head and looked sadly at the lion.

"Would you like to be friends?" asked Lion Ascend.

"What are you doing?" whispered Nikkita.

"I'm having a good heart," he answered.

"Why would you want to be friends with me?" asked Bizare.

"Why not? There comes a time to stand together in times of despair. You don't have to hide in fear," answered Lion Ascend.

"After lived thousands of years and never found my purpose," he answered.

"I'm sorry, but you can live among friends," cracked Lion Ascend.

"I don't think so," replied the dragon.

"That's ok," replied Nikkita as she rose up and walked over to Lion Ascend.

"I hope you know what you're doing," she whispered.

"Let's have fun," replied Lion Ascend as he looked at Iza who looked confused.        "What did you have in mind?" replied Bizare as he noticed Lion Ascend looking at Nikkita who looked as though they knew something he didn't.

# Lion Ascend

The lion, cheetah and the dragon played all day in the trees, the caves and the mountains. Bizare spread his green leathery wings and took flight through the air to see the world. They flew fast and well above the clouds and looked down below to see the mountains. The cats gripped the dragon's thick green scales as the adrenaline rush took hold of them. The dragon flew straight down and heard the two cats screaming, but then Bizare glided horizontally and began laughing. The two cats took deep breaths and were relieved that they were alive. They eventually found themselves back where they started on the mountain with the cave.

Bizare had so much fun he didn't want it to end and neither did Lion Ascend. As all things reveal, nothing lasts forever, not even a day of having fun. LA looked at Iza who looked upset at the wasted day.

"Are you through with playing games?" asked Iza.

"Yes we are," answered Lion Ascend.

"Good because we have much to do," replied Iza.

"Don't we have time to relax? The next test is what? The test of breathing?" asked Lion Ascend with a laugh.

"You should be taking this seriously because you're the last lion in Ayana," declared Iza.

"The last lion?" repeated Bizare as he looked at Lion Ascend. "You really are Lion Ascend! I've heard so many prophetic stories from the Xeras of a courageous lion that will defeat the tigers."

"That's probably what is thought," replied Lion Ascend.

"What is that suppose to mean?" asked Nikkita with a strange look.

"I don't know if I can lead an army against the tigers," answered Lion Ascend.

"You've visited the Burning Bush, climbed the massive mountain, faced the Beast of Speed and still you feel unworthy?" asked the Priest of Pride.

"No, but I feel like a slave," replied Lion Ascend.

"You must complete your training!" said Iza.

The lion turned his head to Bizare; the dragon expressed

amazement with a smile that Lion Ascend possessed the power to lead an army. With a slow gesture from Bizare's

head he knew that he wasn't the only one who felt like a slave to his name. The dragon began to realize who LA really was.

"You believe in me even after I scratched your head to defend myself?" asked Lion Ascend.

"For a long time, I've searched for my purpose. I've killed all who have trespassed, as well as lions, and none have been able to escape. Now that I've learned of your existence from today, I hope that you defeat the tigers," replied Bizare as he picked up the jewel with his mouth, walked into the cave, and disappeared in the darkness.

Lion Ascend felt a strange cold feeling in his back as well as an unsettling feeling of butterflies fluttering in his stomach. The dragon was fueling the young lion with confidence that he never thought he could have. If other lions were killed, then what made him so different? Since he was the last of his kind, he would never know the answer to that question.

"I'm very surprised of the courage you displayed when you asked Bizare to be your friend," said the Priest of Pride as he watched Lion Ascend turn his yellow eyes to the ground.

"I pitied him because I felt his isolation and wanted to comfort him. My enemy is my friend," he said as he rose his head up and looked at the Priest of Pride.

The Priest of Pride nodded, while smiling, as his eyes stared deep into Lion Ascend's. Nikkita felt a warm fuzzy feeling come over her like the wind sweeping through her fur. She felt so happy, but could feel a tear fall upon her cheek, as such words interluded between the two cats.

"You feel the Holy Spirit inside you; the burning fire of inspiration and consciousness, just as the fire from the Burning Bush thrusts its flame unto the sky. You feel it too," cracked Iza as he watched Nikkita drop her jaw.

"Then what about you? I've seen you disappear and reappear, are you real?" asked Lion Ascend.

# Lion Ascend

Iza felt the need to comfort Lion Ascend and Nikkita, "I am as real as you and your friend, just as the feeling of love from the Burning Bush is real. The next challenge is the test of wisdom, you may begin."

Lion Ascend felt the violent shakes of the rocky ground as sand flew through the cracks of the mountains. The sky was as clear as day, the sun shined just the same as yesterday. The power of sand and wind took its effort against the lion in the form of a storm. It spiraled as it took the form of a beast. Lion Ascend knew exactly what he had to do. It was a huge creature that was the size of Bizare, but it was mindless and muscular in stature. After it was completely materialized, it looked at the lion with its black eyes and let out a snarl with its bull like head. Lion Ascend ran to a lower section of the mountains where there was a forest and pond. He ran away from it in great haste to avoid its monstrous jaws. The beast grew a horn from its snout like a rhino and broke through trees and rocks in its haste to destroy the lion. The lion leaped through the air, upon the branches of the trees, to avoid capture by the creature, but felt its wicked thrust as each tree began to fall. Lion Ascend jumped to the branch of another tree, but ended up falling.

With a loud thud to the ground the lion sprang back to his feet and avoided getting killed by the creature which hit another tree. The brute finally realized that it missed its target and bellowed a loud roar before charging again. Lion Ascend spotted a pond far below and ran quickly down the rut and dived in. The fiend pursued the lion and fell in the pond before realizing its fate.

The warm water was nice for an evening swim, but it spelled death for the creature. Lion Ascend watched it run through the water and dematerialize into mud. The beast screamed in horror as it fell to the depths of the pond and into sludge. Lion Ascend won by using his wits and ran back to the top of the plateau to meet Iza. "Congratulations Lion Ascend!" began the Priest of Pride. "You have completed the test of wisdom. The final test involves the challenge of courage, but we'll get to that one tomorrow, now we must sleep," answered Iza as he left to rest.

Lion Ascend took a deep breath and looked to see how peaceful Nikkita was sleeping. He turned around to face the sunset and prayed that he would make it through the next test.

Nikkita woke up and saw Lion Ascend facing the sunset. A smile emerged from her face when she saw his long mane blowing in the wind. The cheetah rose up from the stone floor and slowly walked over to the lion.

"What are you feeling?" she asked while sitting next to him.

"I'm uncertain. Ayana is a big place when you're a child, but soon you realize how small and precious it really is," said Lion Ascend.

"Mother told me something a long time ago. There are two roads in life, love and fear. Everything falls under fear but I feel you will follow love," said Nikkita as she began to smile at Lion Ascend while he turned his head as his eyes met with hers and felt such strength.

"I'm glad you're here with me, I'm glad you're my friend," said Lion Ascend as he watched a full smile emerge on her face.

"I'm your best friend," replied Nikkita as she rose up and walked back to her spot to lie down upon the rock. The cheetah closed her eyes just as she felt something warm lay next to her and smiled again as the thoughts of LA emerged. She turned her head to see it was Lion Ascend lying next to her fast asleep and turned to rest for tomorrow.

Scene 16
1,499

Lion Ascend woke up with a snarl. His eyes were teary eyed as though he lost someone dear. The Burning Bush's warning surfaced within his mind as well as the sight of the tigers and the sight of his old home covered with fire. His mother was the one person that meant the most to him, the one who nurtured him as a child. "Mother!" he cried.

The lion jumped to his feet and stepped forward to the bluffs to watch the sun rise. The sky was purple mixed with red and yellow, which was a pretty mixed up morning for a lion with a lot on his mind. The beauty of the sky made him realize that it wouldn't last long after the tigers desolated the forest and killed all the animals for pleasure rather than for food. It would become ruin, barren and it would fill with a sea of corpse. *Come back home*, the voice of Vera entered his mind. His own voice ordered him; *go back before it's too late.*

Nikkita opened her eyes to the warmth of the sun. Slowly, she raised herself up on her nimble hind legs and stretched her back. The cheetah turned her head to see Lion Ascend at the end of the limestone looking in the distance at the evergreens.

"What's the matter LA?" asked Nikkita as she sat next to him. She was the only one who knew him well enough to discover something was wrong. It would be difficult to not tell her about the vision because it would be hurtful. She was his only close friend and he could not hurt her that way.

"Nikkita what are you doing up?" he asked.

"Wondering why you are up so early," she said with a smile.

"Why do you make things so difficult?" asked Lion Ascend.

"What do you mean?" she asked.

There was a long pause and Lion Ascend spoke to her, "I'm glad you're here.

I'm glad you're my friend."

"Mother told me to watch over you and I plan to keep doing it as long as I can," replied Nikkita.

Lion Ascend looked at her peculiarly, "why?" he asked.

"You are my best friend," she said while gazing into his eyes.

The troubling thought of Vera sent shivers up his spine. Nikkita could sense fear in his heart by the look in his eyes and it made her worry, "is something wrong?"

I'm returning home," answered the mighty lion as he closed both his eyes to hide the tears from Nikkita. The dream of Vera's death scared him.

"What about the next challenge and your destiny!" exclaimed Nikkita as she began following him a couple steps towards the edge of the mountain.

Lion Ascend reopened his eyes as he turned around to look at Nikkita with sadness. "It will have to wait; I had a terrible vision that something bad happened and I must go!"

"What was your vision?" she asked, but he didn't answer, "LA!"

The Priest of Pride watched the leaves rustle and fall into pieces as he watched Lion Ascend run away. The powerful lion took off in a run like no other and felt the thrust of his hind legs push him through the air. He kept thinking of the vision and defied the laws of gravity as he ran down the rugged mountain that he climbed so triumphantly earlier. He felt the over worked sensation of his claws grip the mountain side. Just as he was about to hit the bottom he kicked his hind legs from the mountain and continued to run along the ground. Nikkita's mouth dropped while watching Lion Ascend run down the mountain and turned around to look at the Priest of Pride. She ran past him to take the alternative route to the bottom of the mountain to catch up.

After running for a long time through the woods, Nikkita realized she had caught up with Lion Ascend and was keeping up just fine. Flashbacks unfolded from Lion Ascend's past that he had learned from Vera of what it was to have a good heart. She protected him from danger and took him in as her own. He owed his life to Vera and would die to protect her.

Before long, they reached the den and Lion Ascend felt a sad and dreadful feeling come over him. Nikkita took a quick halt as Lion Ascend froze in his tracks. Mother cheetah was lying on the ground and was not moving. They saw Chalice and Lobby nuzzle up to her, but she didn't respond. As LA and Nikkita came closer, they could see wounds on her neck and body with blood soaked in her fur. Nikkita nuzzled up to her mother and began to cry.

"Get up, get up," she repeated, but there was no word and the silence began to weigh heavily on the cats.

Lion Ascend turned around and walked away because it was more than he could handle. A flashback entered such mind when he was young and remembered the promise he made to protect her.

He wanted to escape the pain, but didn't know how. The great lion turned to see his siblings grieving for their mother. After running away, he felt alone and couldn't sit to deal with his regret of not being around to protect her. He let out a loud bellow of anger in the sound of a roar and could hear it echo everywhere. He ripped apart every tree with the strength of his claws. He was angry, sad, and wanted justice with the one who did this. "Lion Ascend!" At first he thought it was Vera, but he was mistaken. He turned around to see it was Nikkita and realized that she was not coming back.

"It's my fault," he began. "I promised to protect her and I failed!" His voice trembled as he backed up two steps while shaking his head.

"There is no blame in this," began Nikkita. "Think of all she taught you! To have a good heart," she sobbed ". . . and think about what you're going to do next," continued Nikkita. "Sure it was a bad thing that happened, but don't forget she was my mother too and I would have died for her."

There was a moment of silence before Nikkita spoke again and she rubbed her face into his. "There is one thing you can do. You can pursue what she wanted you to have, which is to have a good heart. You can call all the animals and inspire us to fight for freedom. That's what she would have wanted. Many of us can't hunt to feed ourselves without being threatened by the tigers. Some of us feel hopeless and without hope we will die!" cried Nikkita.

Lion Ascend nodded his head as his whitish gold aura began to appear around his body. He realized what the Burning Bush was talking about and knew what to do.

He let out a roar that could be heard for miles around Everlow. Seconds turned to minutes and there was nothing but the echoes of the loud bellow vibrating from his vocal cords. The brightness of the sun pierced through the clouds and shined upon Lion Ascend as though it heard him.

The lion turned around to Nikkita who slowly smiled as parts of his mane brushed near his eyes. He was sad and only faith could bring them through this darkness. Nikkita continued to smile as her eyes began to open wide. She knew something powerful was happening and all they needed to do was wait.

The sound of her voice gave Lion Ascend the confidence he needed. He took off in a run and jumped on a large boulder near by where he let out one last roar for all the animals in the distance to hear. With that roar, flashbacks entered his mind of Vera and all the good that was left in Everlow.

Lion Ascend and Nikkita walked back to the den where Vera's body lay. Abel charged in, with his huge number of wolves, to see what had happened. Enoch glided to the ground, as well, to see the sadness that everyone was feeling. The Priest of Pride walked slowly through the forest of Everlow to witness the moment of silence and knew what was going on.

The animals looked sad at what was lost, but suddenly something magical happened. A huge number of animals began massing in Everlow. Leopards, black panthers, rhinoceros, wooly mammoths, elephants, wild horses, zebras, elk, moose, wart hogs, badgers, wolverines and fox all grouped to see Lion Ascend. The lion could hardly believe his eyes and wondered if he was dreaming. This was the answer to his roar and hundreds of animals came to him because of the call he made, as well as, the prophecy that had been passed on through the years. A fragile smile emerged upon Lion Ascend's face as he saw more and more animals of all different species coming to his aide.

Chalice and Lobby buried Vera next to the den as more animals began to emerge to see Lion Ascend. Abel looked around to see the large number of animals and felt a wave of assurance to take on the tigers. The threat of the tigers had been a constant reminder of death and they wouldn't give up the Bad Lands easily. Lion Ascend nodded as he looked at the pile of dirt that buried Vera. He could still remember everything about her from the moment he was a cub to the time he watched her defend him from Jezebel. Slowly, he pushed the dirt from side to side with his big paw and allowed Nikkita, Lobby and Chalice to put their paw prints upon the dirt.

Minutes passed and the lion began sniffing the ground around the den. He was looking for any clues of the killer. The forest was silent with no chirping of birds or the sound of crickets. It was as though the creatures of the forest knew what Lion Ascend was thinking.

"Lion Ascend," began General Abel. "Look at the huge number of souls that are here to stand with you!"

Lion Ascend halted his smell and looked around to see the animal's hopeful eyes. He could see their desperate desire to have a strong leader help them end the darkness and lead them to the light. He was their leader and they needed him.

A stir of confusion consumed Lobby as he stepped forward. "She's been dead for a while," replied Lobby as Lion Ascend looked at him.

"We need you to fight the tigers with us. Will you help us?" asked Chalice.

There was a moment of silence between the lion and his brother. Lion Ascend knew that Vera's departure hurt Chalice, but he wanted to stand with his brother against the forces of evil and free the land.

"I want to know who killed her," answered Lion Ascend. There had to be a way to find out who did this. There was no scent because it had rained, but perhaps inside the den there would be clues. The lion looked at the small narrow hole and knew that he wouldn't be able to fit inside. With a nudge of his head he gestured General Abel to investigate. "Who ever killed my mother must have gone into the den as well."

"Very well sir," replied the general as he stepped through the hole. Minutes went by and Lion Ascend looked at his siblings and sensed their pain from the expression on their faces. He saw Nikkita crying as she nuzzled up to Lobby for comfort. The white wolf returned from their sacred place with sadness in his eyes and with a slow shake of his head and looked at Lion Ascend, "A tiger killed her."

"Who?" demanded Lion Ascend.

"I don't know," replied Abel.

The great lion felt a wave of anger run through his body. He knew that the animals needed him just from the look in their eyes. Maybe he wouldn't take the life of Vera's killer, but he would definitely seek justice for the brave souls that surrounded him. It was such a deep undertaking and wondered if he would have the courage to see it through. Every animal that he passed called his name and it made his heart quicken with strength. Lion Ascend looked at Nikkita as her eyes looked into his eyes, "why do they call my name?" he asked.

"Because they have nowhere to go and they believe you are their leader," Nikkita answered as she watched him take a deep breath and a few minutes went by before he made a move.

"All right everybody! I need each and every one of you to join me in a fight against the tigers. There is a chance you or your comrade next to you may die today. That is why, I implore you to protect each other and put up a fight that the tigers will never forget. This is our land! We have the right to be here! We have the right to be alive!" roared Lion Ascend. With that he heard a loud applause of howls, cheers and grunts.

"And so it begins," whispered General Abel as he watched Lion Ascend approach him.

"Mobilize every wolf to the Bad Lands, I'm leading the attack!" Lion Ascend ordered as he let out a roar and charged to the west followed by animals of all sizes.

High in the air Jezebel was scouting the edge of Everlow with the ravens and crows. He watched with great concern at the large mass of animals moving towards the Bad Lands and to Death Mountain where Tyrone ruled. Jezebel had to warn Tyrone that they would be under attack in a matter of hours. The large number of birds culled and flew quickly to their master.

Lion Ascend led the rebellion to the edge of the woods just before the plains with the Bad Lands ahead and let out a roar to any other animals in the area to join them. The time had come for the cleansing of the land and to take back what was stolen. The wooly mammoths broke through the trees and dead branches quickly as they followed their leader. They made way for many of the smaller animals like the wolverines, badgers and foxes to get through. The zebras, elk, wolves, cheetahs, leopards and wild cats kept up with Lion Ascend. Soon the animals passed the great cat and were racing onward to the Bad Lands. It felt exhilarating and powerful to see all the animals stand together with him.

Lion Ascend stopped to inspire the animals to continue and turned around to the white wolf. "It's hard to believe how rich our numbers have grown!" said General Abel confidently. Lion Ascend smiled at him and remembered what the Burning Bush told him. "Someone once told me that someday I would be great and I would not always have all the answers, but I believe that everyone should have the right to be free! I thank you for fighting for me to live," declared Lion Ascend with a smile. "It was an honor my lord, thank you for giving us this day to watch you in your glory," replied the white wolf.

The great cat nodded and began running with Abel at his side to catch up with the animals in the front. Their numbers were still strong, but suddenly the lion was watching a huge number of eagles and albatrosses glide through the sky. The great lion knew that a great power was emerging against the forces of evil.

"You're telling me that a huge number of animals are heading this way to attack?" growled Tyrone as he rose from his throne to stare at Cain, Talick and Jezebel who were afraid that they would be killed.

"What are we going to do my lord?" asked Cain.

I'm going to feed your dead carcass to the lion that you were suppose to kill when he was a child!" There was silence until the growl of a tiger came running into the throne room. "Sir, there is an army massing in the east, the biggest army I've ever seen!"

Tyrone looked at the tiger and then at Cain. "If this lion wants a war then we shall give him one. Cain, mobilize the hyenas! Talick, gather all the coyotes and jackals that haven't left to go hunting!" What should I do?" asked Jezebel. "You are going to go with them and assemble the rest of the crows, ravens and hawks.

Don't fail me!" ordered Tyrone. The crow nodded and took off through the air to assemble his followers.

In the distance, from Death Mountain, three-hundred tigers were waiting for the rebellion. The Bad Lands was perfect camouflage for the tigers to attack. About a hundred hyenas, coyotes and jackals joined the tigers at the front line. The sound of volcanoes rang through their ears as well as the sound of ravens and crows piercing the sky with their calls. Cain and Talick nodded their heads to the general with respect to signal that they were ready. "The wind is blowing in their direction. They will know that we are here waiting for them," said Cain. "They out number us," warned Jezebel. "You exaggerate, I sent my fastest rider to ask Prince Voltar to assemble a thousand tigers to assist us against this rebellion. We must find a way to intimidate the lion and the animals before they come to Death Mountain," replied General Cabass. Just then they heard a loud roar in the distance and knew Lion Ascend was near. The rebellion had entered the Bad Lands

Lion Ascend let out another roar as all the animals stood behind him. He knew the tigers were just beyond the path to the Bad Lands. They were in a meadow and could see the mountains straight ahead. The wind carried the scent of tigers all the way to his nose. The sun shined brightly in the sky while pebbles and rocks fell along the mountain side. Lion Ascend suspected they were being spied on because he saw birds fly from where the pebbles fell. His brothers, sister and general stood next to him. With only the sound of breathing from the animals, a great temptation to rush the tigers soon subsided. He let out another roar, "Come out cowards, let justice be done to you!"

Time stood still as Lion Ascend sniffed the air. The sun was bright over head and without a breeze Abel panted to keep cool. Lion Ascend's eyebrows began to protrude as he squinted at the sight of a small band of animals walking towards him. A tiger and three wild dogs were walking slowly towards them. A gust of wind suddenly blew into Lion Ascend's face and the clouds veiled the sun as the lion walked to meet their enemies in the middle of the small meadow. Nikkita, General Abel, Lobby, Enoch and

Chalice joined the lion and wondered what was going to happen next. Soon they came to a stop and were eye to eye with the tiger, Cain, Talick and jackal.

"Such a beautiful day," began the tiger with a sneer.

"I'm General Cabass, the highest general under Lord Tyrone, my dear lion," said the tiger

"You will not address him as lion!" exclaimed Nikkita. "He is Lion Ascend, the highest servant to the Burning Bush and your king of Ayana!" There was a huge bellow of laughter from the tiger and his comrades that made Nikkita upset.

Lion Ascend's face was like stone; he knew who he was and nobody would tell him different. General Abel began to growl until he heard the great lion hush the white wolf's burning anger. They saw General Cabass' army come out from behind the mountains slowly.

"So this is the king of Everlow?" continued Cabass in laughter.

"The true king of our world Ayana, he is your king," added General Abel after General Cabass stopped laughing.

"We're prepared to fight," ordered Cabass. "Leave," growled Cain.

"You're bluffing," Chalice growled back.

"You mock us?" exclaimed Cain. "Maybe you should hide in your mother's hole where she died!" exclaimed General Cabass.

"Our mother died so we could live!" cried Nikkita. ". . . . And I would die for her," added Lobby.

"These lands belong to the tigers," declared General Cabass.

All of a sudden Lion Ascend let out a roar that silenced everybody and blew an unfriendly gust of wind into the tiger's face. "These lands belong to the animals that stand behind me. You will disband your army and leave!" ordered Lion Ascend with a growl.

"Who do you think you are?" asked the tiger.

"I am Lion Ascend!"

Before anyone realized it, General Cabass charged at the

great cat and began clawing with all his might. The tigers and creatures, from behind, charged to attack. Jezebel squawked in anger as he flew from the sky and tried to rip out the lion's eyes with his deadly claws. Lion Ascend, while pinned down by the tiger, watched in horror just as Enoch swooped up from the ground and attacked Jezebel. Lion Ascend thrust the tiger off of him and swiped his claws across the cat's face.

Nikkita looked into the distance, to the west, to see hundreds of tigers, hyenas, jackals, coyotes and a mist of birds drawing close. She turned to the east and saw their great army of animals charging against the opposing army. The cheetah looked up; the birds battled each other. Her siblings, as well as Abel, were fighting Cain, Talick and the jackal. She realized this would be a battle that would not be forgotten.

Lion Ascend ripped the tiger's chest and opened his mouth to grip the enemy's head. Cabass squirmed and fought, but could not break free. With the close of his deadly jaws, Lion Ascend thrust his enemy to the ground and realized that he had killed him.

LA turned his head to see the battle unfold before his eyes. The three cheetahs saved Abel's life from Cain and kept executing their fury upon the hyena. The wild dogs unleashed themselves upon the incoming wolves. A stampede of wooly mammoths and wild horses trampled through the mighty line of tigers and allowed the wolverines, badgers and wild cats a chance to fight. Lion Ascend ran deftly through the battle followed by a few number of animals. His objective was to find Lord Tyrone and face him to end the war.

After running a long time through the path around the mountains, Lion Ascend stopped to see who was with him. It was Nikkita, Chalice, Lobby, a wolverine and a fox. The lion listened to hear the sounds of howls from the wolves as well as the tigers roaring.

"We're with you," boasted the fox.

"Who might you be?" asked Lion Ascend.

"My name is Cox and my friend's name is---"

"Way," interrupted the wolverine.

"Well Way and Cox try to keep up," he answered as he took off in a run like no other.

The last twenty tigers at Death Mountain smelled Lion Ascend's scent. As Lord Tyrone walked outside the entrance he could see the fear in the tiger's eyes. "My lord, he is coming to kill us all," cried one of the tigers.

"Who?" asked Tyrone.

"The lion that was foretold to save the animals," said another.

"Don't bother, I'm already here!" exclaimed Lion Ascend as he walked towards the group of tigers.

"Kill them," ordered Tyrone as he walked back inside the cave to his dark throne. The tigers began to group together to protect the entrance against the lion.

"LA! Don't," said Nikkita as she stopped him.

"Let us fight with you," replied Chalice.

"Let us stand with you and laugh in their faces!" roared Way.

"I appreciate you standing beside me, but I can feel the will of the Burning Bush answer my dream, wish and prayer. We don't need to fight any longer," answered Lion Ascend as he left his friends behind and began walking towards the tigers.

The lion looked at the large group of tigers and saw fear in their eyes; fear that had been taught to them since they were cubs by a much greater evil. Lion Ascend closed his eyes and concentrated on his visit from the Burning Bush.

*Oh great Burning Bush, give me the strength to carry on. Grant me the foresight to know what I must do from the depths of Everlow to the Valley of Evil. Build me a wall for my enemy and give me a path to enter. For I am Lion Ascend your Holy Servant.*

Lion Ascend opened his eyes as he felt the tiger's darkened aura. "You're not getting through," growled one of the tigers.

---

"You're troubled my friend," began Lion Ascend.

"I'm not your friend. You're from a weak lineage of lions and you shall parish with the rest," roared the tiger as he was about to charge.

Just then without a warning, a burst of fire thrust its way through the ground and surrounded the lion. The tigers stepped aside as Lion Ascend walked past them and into the cave and the fire moved to surround the tigers. Nikkita led the way, for her brothers and friends to stand with the lion.

The fire flickered from the magma leaving the cave in shadows. It was dark and humid for the lion, but he remained silent as he watched the silhouette of Tyrone walk towards him. Tyrone emerged with a stick in his mouth that had fire on the end. He lit the red liquid on fire. It was six feet wide and surrounded him and Lion Ascend in a circle of fire. The tiger stared at the lion with death in his eyes and waited for the invader to come closer.

The cheetahs could see that Lion Ascend was trapped with the leader of the tigers and might fall to his death. They were his friends and wanted to fight by his side to the very end. Lion Ascend turned his head to see his friend and felt he had strength of confidence that he never had before.

"You don't have to do this!" exclaimed Nikkita.

"We can all gang up on him!" assured Chalice.

"No, I have to do this," declared Lion Ascend. The great cat's thoughts were silent except with the voices of Iza and Vera speaking to him in his mind. "Have a good heart. Face yourself in the test of courage." The words echoed with such agility and comfort that it sent his worries away like the dawn of the sun after a deadly storm.

"You can't expect me to believe that one lion is going to stand a chance against the power of the empire," bellowed Tyrone.

Lion Ascend stepped closer to Tyrone and sat down as an idea emerged for peace. "I challenge you, one on one. I have one condition and that is the loser is allowed to live. If you lose, you leave and never return," replied Lion Ascend.

"If I lose, I will leave," said Lion Ascend. The tiger scoffed and was eager to tear the lion to shreds. "My condition as conqueror is we fight to the death!" Lion Ascend looked at Tyrone with fear and knew that he would have to fight and protect himself.

Lion Ascend felt the breath of the tiger's mighty bellow turn his veins into ice. The tiger lifted his upper lip and protruded his eyebrows to intimidate his adversary. Lion Ascend looked deep into the tiger's eyes and heard the Burning Bushes' voice in his head. *You won't fail because I will be there by your side.*

"To the death!" yelled Tyrone.

Tyrone was smaller than Lion Ascend, but he was experienced, quick and vicious. The tiger swung his claws, striking the lion's face and shed blood. The lion felt the blood drip from his forehead and near his right eye. The tiger charged to inflict his worse destruction to rip the lion apart. Lion Ascend let out a roar in pain and hit the tiger with all his might. He opened his jaws onto Tyrone's throat and scratched the tiger's face with his claws. After seconds the two cats split apart to catch their breath before realizing what they were going to do next.

"Come on LA!" yelled Nikkita. The cats, wolverine and fox began to chant his name louder and faster.

"You're suppose to be Lion Ascend, King of Everlow!" laughed Tyrone "Well let me tell you something, you're nothing. I'm the one who killed your mother!" exclaimed Tyrone as he watched Lion Ascend flatten his ears and glare at him with anger. "Yea, I killed your mother, the disgusting recourse of a female dog who was in no form a reputable animal to give mercy to. She's nothing, all your friends here are nothing, and your friends out there are nothing!" Lion Ascend revealed his teeth while he looked at Tyrone with disgust and became very angry.

Deep inside the heart of the great cat was the anger that unleashed at the one who killed Vera. Lion Ascend gritted his teeth and let out a loud roar, which propelled him a reason to live and continue fighting. The lion charged at the tiger; He began clawing and biting the tiger with all his might. Lion Ascend ripped the tiger's ear off and left open wounds that spilled blood deep into his enemy's fur as well as around the neck. He swatted his paw across the tiger's face leaving scratch marks, but the final blow resulted when Lion Ascend hit the tiger so hard that Tyrone was knocked back fifteen feet just inches from the magma. Tyrone remained motionless with bits and pieces of soil and blood in his mouth. Lion Ascend stood before the tiger, quiet and patient. He wondered what would become of Tyrone if he would submit.

"Surrender, it's over," he commanded.

Tyrone got up slowly, his legs twitched and he stumbled to the ground. He could barely stand on his feet, but forced himself to walk even though he was exhausted. He didn't want Lion Ascend to get the best of him and wanted to finish the fight.

"I will never surrender!" exclaimed Tyrone as he watched Lion Ascend begin walking towards him.

"The land belongs to all the animals who want to live in peace and have freedom. Kneel before me as your servant and join us against Prince Voltar as well as the forces of evil," ordered Lion Ascend. Tyrone spit blood at the lion with disgust because he didn't want to surrender.

All of a sudden, General Abel walked in with about twenty wolves and Lion Ascend turned his head to the general with a smile. The battle was over and Death Mountain was now under the control of Lion Ascend and his army.

"What's going on?" Abel whispered to Nikkita, but he received no answer.

"Remember all that you have done to the land and all that you stole from the
animals? You have brought great evil upon yourself and to this peaceful world. You killed an innocent mother who only wished to live," declared Lion Ascend.

Tyrone looked into the lion's eyes and the cheetah while seeing himself tremble with shame. He had committed sin and felt he deserved to die, but Lion Ascend wouldn't kill him. Tyrone was so close to death that he could touch it with the grace of his paw. Then it came to him, as the sound of bubbling could be heard and the sight of liquid fire could be seen spooling out before him. Without another word, Tyrone turned and jumped into the hot magma. Tyrone felt the burning sensation throughout his body and embraced death.

Lion Ascend closed his eyes for it was not what he wanted. The great cat turned around and was about to exit the cave when Abel stopped him. "The battle is over! The tigers are running away deeper in the mountains. Should we pursue them?"

"No, let them go! Word shall spread quickly to Voltar that I have arrived to set right, to what once was wrong," answered Lion Ascend as he stepped through the crowd of wolves and walked outside to find the tigers held by the walls of fire. The huge number of animals that were around, were waiting for his command. With a slight nod of respect to his new friends, they relaxed and nodded to him. "What should we do with the prisoners?" asked Chalice. Lion Ascend turned his head around to the white wolf that emerged from the darkness, with the pack of wolves behind him. Nikkita looked into Lion Ascend's eyes and saw the kindness unleashed from such heart. He was more than what the animals of Everlow wanted. With the close of his eyes he commanded the fire to renounce itself from the ground, "sacred flame renounce yourself to the ground for I'm Lion Ascend." The fire disappeared from around the tigers.

"Let the tigers go," commanded Lion Ascend to Chalice.

"What!" exclaimed Chalice.

"We're going to release them," replied Lion Ascend as he walked towards the twenty tigers and watched them look at him with fear. "You're free to go, tell your master that I have spared your life," he commanded as he watched them run away.

"No thank you, no gratitude and no apologies," said Abel smiling and shaking his head.

"Why did you let them go?" asked Way.

Lion Ascend was silent and knew that there were no words to describe why he was doing this. "We've won this battle for Everlow, but we still have a war to win Ayana. He walked over to the ledge as he heard Sampson howl. "We've won! Let us celebrate our victory with grace!" howled Knightly.

Upon the highest mountain, near Death Mountain, Iza and

Dafidale watched the celebration and saw the lion walk towards the end of the cliff. The wind brushed up against Dafidale's skin as she looked at Iza who was very pleased by the outcome of the battle. A hundred little lightning bugs flew in circles around the Queen of the Xeras.

"Look Priest of Pride, the prophecy has come at last, Lion Ascend has defeated the tigers!" she exclaimed with a wondrous smile.

"He still has a long way to go," replied the Priest of Pride.

"If heroes, blessed with such greatness, are given the chance to bring love to the
world what will become of us?" she asked.

"Nothing, for he needs us now more than ever-"     "Wait" interrupted Dafidale as she watched Nikkita trot to the lion.

Lion Ascend sat on the mountain to watch the sunset and felt the bitterness of his wounds. It was a reminder of what was lost as well as what was gained, but soon he would be faced against Prince Voltar and would have new wounds to bare. He looked troubled about something and looked to see Nikkita.

"What's the matter, LA?" asked Nikkita. "All the cats are celebrating the return of the land."

"I don't deserve to celebrate, for I have killed Tyrone," replied Lion Ascend as he lowered his head in shame.

"LA, that wasn't your fault," began Nikkita. "He was trying to kill you and you gave him mercy because you have a good heart," Nikkita answered while healing his wounds with a kiss upon his forehead. It felt good and sweet like rain sprinkling from the sky.

"Come with me," Nikkita teased as she ran away from him.

"Nikkita!" yelled Lion Ascend as he picked up a yellow rose from the side of the bluff. She stopped to turn around and see him looking upon her with fondness as he dropped it to her feet.

"I'm glad you're here and I'm glad you're my friend."

"I will always be your friend," she replied and nuzzled her nose upon his and smiled. Suddenly, she saw a large heart made up of the lightning bugs.

The words inside it spelled out; HAVE A GOOD HEART.
She became giddy with unstoppable laughter; Lion Ascend turned
around to see what there was to laugh about. When he saw the sign
he joined Nikkita in loving laughter for he new he really did have a
good heart. The sun finally set behind the mountains, leaving the
animals to rest assured that tomorrow would bring hope, peace and
happiness.

## **The Author's Thank You List**

I would like to thank my sisters (my strongest support and inspiration); Ariane, Stephanie, Kayla, dad and mom. Special thanks to Debbie (I really appreciate your help, I couldn't have gotten this far without you) and Stan. I would also like to thank my grandma, aunts uncles and my cousins for your support. I would like to Thank Melissa and Maureen for reading my poems from "What I Think About You" and your supportive constructive criticism to continue to be creative. I would like to thank Kisus Metoxen (best friend and pen pal), Corinne (Cheetah) (for teaching and showing me what it means to give hugs and believe in your dreams), I would also like to thank my friends at Pizza Hut, and UPS for reading older versions of this story and inspiring me to keep going with it and my other books; Linda Mancheski (The best RGM manager I've ever had) , Marry and Marty Fagnan(for reading my works) , and  Mike Van Ness (for telling me I've got a gift). I would also like to thank, Robert Harris (for getting me inspired in my first novel), Lisa Hildebrandt (for falling in love with me as a person and what I write), Mrs. Murphy(for encouraging me in writing), Lisa Steiner(for loving me even though I didn't do a good job at loving you back), Mr. Frautschi (believing I can do anything), Naomi Pidd(for the experience of waiting until you get married and reading my work), Mrs. Erickson(inspiring me with my novel), Mrs. Klass(for helping me succeed in my dreams and I have), Mary Olson(helping me find God and I found God in 2002), Alice Stout (being nice to me when nobody else was), Jeff Hanson (encouraging me to write music), Cheryl Boden(teaching me my sixth sense), Gabe Wahl(scaring the bullies away and being a friend), Duane Standard (helping and inspiring me to write and find romance), Duane Martinson (sitting next to me while I was writing my songs and encouraging me to write), Chris Lee (showing me how to draw Garfield in 2nd grade, which led to writing), Ms. Bongers (siding with me against the kids at school that would pick on me and encourage me to continue writing my novel), Mrs. Driscol (for telling a student to leave me alone who was picking on me and wouldn't leave me alone) Angie Rivard (a huge encouragement to accept who I am), Mr. Rivard (showing optimism in my strength in running and writing, Mrs. Quiling(letting me play all day and create), Mrs. Refsnyder (the best first grade teacher I've ever had), Mrs. Eck(showing me short cuts in learning), Jeff and Rob Pierson (Two brothers who made me feel like a brother, thank you) , Ms. Morse, (for reading my novel) Mrs. Belisle (for reading my novel) Shannon Barkley (a good friend who gave me memorable experiences to write about, Deb Zeilsdorf (for making me laugh when I was down), Dave Hanson (for reading my stories and leading me to God) , Freddy Henzler (a huge inspiration for writing, drawing and seeing the good in everyone), Karin Dillner (making me laugh and feel special at "Arts World"), Stephanie Grimm (for inspiring me to illustrate and experience the attitude of someone young), Kathy Kleinhans, (for encouraging me to continue writing and to not stop) Cathy Garbe (for getting me interested in the writing school and giving me excellent feed back on my stories), Jeremy Gilbert (for your expertise to choose the right college that led to being more creative), Dave Herr(your encouragement to being creative), Darren Corbin (motivating me to go for my dreams), Mrs. Irlebeck (getting me interested in writing in 3rd grade), Dave Hunt, (for seeing me as the good person that I am as well as writing and one of the reason I joined basketball in 8th grade) Keith Moyer (for being my best friend in Junior High and part of high school and kicking *ss on TMNT Arcade), Craig Peterson (for encouraging me to continue writing), Darlyn Thomas (for your enlightenment to see that everyone is intelligent), Lori Johnson (for the article on publishing), Jay Fletch (for teaching me how to draw in 5th grade it really helped motivate me in writing), Trautmiller family; Freddy, Timmy and Matt (my neighbors) (had a lot of fun 4-

wheeling, pool, fools ball, playing football, basketball, baseball and for Freddy who got me started on the first paragraph of my novel, thanks), Chad Hill (for being a good friend and influence), Robert Norton (for leading me to Kristy and telling me I need to write and get my stories published), Adrian Bravo (with his amazing illustrations), Trent Landry (for inspiring me to join Trek, but also that a man can accomplish anything when he tries hard enough) and the Landry family for visiting and supporting my last book signing.

I would like to thank my friends at McDonalds and Goodwill for your support in my dreams and everyone that was a huge influence, but aren't mentioned. You know who you are.

Artist I would like to thank that inspire to write; Starship, Jane Siberry, Michael W. Smith, Nycole Nordeman, Bryan Adams and Mozart Celtic. I thank you.

I would like to thank my friends at the news paper; The Hudson Star Observer, Doug, Julia from the New Richmond Paper, The Stillwater Gazette, The Tri-County Paper and Norma from the Somerset Library.

A special thanks to *graphic designer* Theresa Bliven; I would like to say thanks for your encouragement and expertise for the cover design, art, cover design and illustration for the book, thank you.

A special thanks to the people who read in my work shop and gave me feed back to this book while I continued to revise for the last ten years.

Linda and Miles Narveson
Dan Aluni of Mystic Suns
Erica Fuss
Mary and Mary Fagnan
Cathy Paguin

## Synopsis's

In the world of Ayana the lions protected the land and the innocent from evil. Evil emerged with the rise of the tigers who built an empire and over powered the lions by killing the bravest and strongest lions in their sleep. The elder lions were killed and the youngest lions were pushed into a giant mirror called the catacomb.

A prophecy was passed generation after generation for a thousand years. This prophecy that emerged was about Lion Ascend. At this point the animals of Copper Toe lost hope for life as well as freedom and began to join the empire of the tigers. Great sadness loomed with the animals, but some built an underground resistance against the empire. The resistance finally challenged the tiger's empire, but after months of fighting the resistance failed.

Lion Ascend was created from the Ascending Realms and brought by the Burning Bush. Iza the Priest of Pride encourages Vera, the cheetah, to take Lion Ascend as her own. Vera reluctantly takes him and teaches him how to be kind, loving and merciful.

Lion Ascend discovers after he grows up that he is the last lion. The Burning Bush and Dafidale tell him he has been chosen to unite the animals of the world against the empire of the tigers. Unsure of who he is, he feels the pressure directed to him by Iza and General Abel to be great. He learns what love is from Nikkita and the true meaning of what it is to have a good heart.

With the help of his friends he sets off on a journey to uncover his identity of the future. To reclaim the courage of what the lions held to bring unity and freedom in the land against evil. Join Lion Ascend on his journey and find

Lion Ascend

out if he finds his courage to defeat the tigers.

## About the Author

Ryan Keith Johnson was born in Stillwater, Minnesota and grew up in Somerset Wisconsin. He got interested in writing when he was in third grade. After writing short stories in fourth and fifth grade for school projects he began writing his first novel when he was in sixth grade and finished in seventh grade.

In 2007 he wrote and published "The King's Retribution". In 2008 he wrote and published "Strip Me Of My Gold," which was published in Immortal Versus. In 2011, "What I Think About you" was published. The book was a collection of song lyrics and poetry written from the last eighteen years of his life.

The writer is different than most authors because he puts himself in his characters. His creative, innovative and high energy allows him to go further in his writing than his last project.

The author enjoys listening to music, watching movies and making new friends with creative people. To get him inspired he enjoys listening to Celtic, Classical, Christian rock and some heavy metal bands. He is still writing and is working on new writing projects to be completed and published soon.